Magically Delicious

CURSE OF THE ARCHANGELS

JAYLEE AUSTIN

Moira's magic potion for love

A spoonful of honeycombs
One cup of thyme of romance,
A zest of orange tenderness,
Two cups of compatible flour,
Half a cup of humorous lavender,
Two heaps of sugar kisses,
A strudel of cinnamon passion,
A pinch of sweet laughter of mint.

Moria's crumb cake

CRUMB CAKE RECIPE FROM
BAKINGAMOMENT.COM

Crumb Cake Muffins

Prep Time

25 mins

Cook Time

17 mins

Total Time

42 mins

Tender sour cream coffee cake, ribboned with cinnamon and topped with a crumbly streusel topping. These crumb cake muffins are a great way to start the day!

Course: Breakfast, Brunch, Snack

Cuisine: American

Keyword: coffee cake muffin recipe, coffee cake muffins, Crumb Cake, Crumb Cake Muffins

Servings: 12 muffins

Calories: 459 kcal

Ingredients

For the cinnamon crumb topping

• 1/2 cup (1 stick) unsalted butter, melted

- 1 1/2 cups <u>all-purpose flour</u>
- 1/2 cup packed light brown sugar
- 2 teaspoons <u>ground cinnamon</u>
- 1/4 teaspoon <u>kosher salt</u>

For the sour cream coffee cake muffins

- 3 cups <u>all-purpose flour</u>
- 1 cup <u>granulated sugar</u>
- 1 tablespoon <u>baking powder</u>
- 1/4 teaspoon <u>kosher salt</u>
- 1/2 cup (1 stick) unsalted butter, melted
- 1 cup sour cream
- 3 tablespoons milk
- 2 large eggs
- 1 1/2 teaspoons <u>vanilla extract</u>

Instructions

To make the cinnamon crumb topping:

1 Toss the melted butter, flour, brown sugar, cinnamon, and salt together with a fork until crumbly.

To make the sour cream coffee cake muffins:

1 Preheat the oven to 425 degrees F and line a muffin pan with papers.

2 Place the flour, sugar, baking powder, and salt in a large bowl and whisk to combine.

3 In a smaller bowl, whisk the melted butter, sour cream, milk, eggs, and vanilla together until smooth.

4 Add the sour cream mixture to the dry ingredients, and fold together until just barely combined.

5 Fill the wells of the muffin pan halfway with the sour cream coffee cake batter, then top with a few teaspoons of the cinnamon crumb topping.

6 Divide the remaining batter equally among all 12 wells of the muffin pan, and top with the remaining cinnamon crumb topping.

7 Bake the crumb cake muffins for 5 minutes at 425 degrees F, then turn the oven temperature down to 350 degrees F and continue to bake for 14 to 18 minutes, or until a toothpick inserted in the thickest part of a muffin comes out clean or with a few moist crumbs.

Recipe Notes

More great muffin recipes:

• <u>Morning Glory Muffins</u>

The Sarim Curse

The Curse

Yahweh and Diablo once ruled in harmony, Yahweh over the spiritual part of the universe and Diablo over the physical aspect of it. However, a rebellion by Diablo sparked a war between Yahweh's loyal angels and Diablo's demons. Lucifer disagreed with the separation of power and led his supporters in defiance of Yahweh's rule.

The angelic wars caused great losses for Yahweh, including the departure of his beloved wife to live within the mortal realm. He cursed five of his sons for fighting alongside Lucifer. As punishment, he exiled their females away from Kumuria to live among the fae domains.

The protection of their archeia was of utmost importance. So, the powerful Fates scattered the precious chakra stones of the kundalini dragon, which represented all living beings. Today,

humanity struggles to maintain a delicate balance between feminine and masculine energies.

To break this curse, each chosen prince must embark on a journey to recover the scattered chakra stones of their beloved archeia's soul and undo the destructive damage caused by Yahweh's curse. It is only after they have accomplished this quest that we can hope for harmony and balance in our world.

As time flew by, the memory of the curse sank into oblivion. But fate had something else in store; a mysterious force appeared from the shadows aiming to overpower all realms. Thankfully, the Sarim Archangel Princes, who could stop the endless darkness, still held the power to save the universe.

To reach this goal, they must first find their soulmates, the archeia, and unite their spirits, so they can defeat the malicious entities. Time is running out, and the future of the mortal realm hangs in the balance, resting on the prince's shoulders. It is essential that all five succeed; if even one fails, it could mean disaster for humanity for thousands of years. Plus the true death of the archangel's soul.

Chapter One

URIEL CONNER

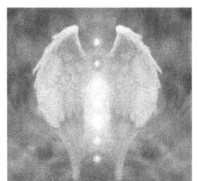

Sunlight poured through the leafy canopy outside my loft's bay window, dancing in warm slivers across the hardwood floor. I pressed my palm against the cool glass and sensed the shift in the air. Something was coming. My other hand drifted to the jagged scar over my heart. A dull ache whispered memories of Aurora, my spirit-mate banished to Earth, and for a heartbeat I tasted the hollow of loss, never to experience the passion of genuine love.

Behind me, Luc's footsteps tapped on the polished plank. "Coffee?" he offered, voice low as gravel.

I turned, shrugged into my tie. "Yeah."

He set down a steaming mug and leaned against the windowsill. "Diablo was at Tartarus's gate last night."

My throat tightened. "What did that bastard want?"

Luc lifted his eyebrows. "Our father and uncle are locked in a tug-of-war over human souls."

I pinched the bridge of my nose. "Naturally."

Luc sipped his coffee, turned on the TV to a weather report. "Diablo wants you to lose to Samael."

I stared at the mug as if it held a poison. Losing had never occurred to me. I closed my eyes and sent a thought-pulse to Samael. "You're slipping, brother. Still carrying your tail between your legs and doing what Diablo demands?"

A low laugh in my skull. Samael's voice coiled inside my skull like a snake. "You still think the old man's favorite can keep up? My, my, Uriel. You never could take a joke."

The taunt affected my confidence more sharply than glass. I bit back the urge to retaliate, knowing his psychic barbs were bait. "You should worry less about me and more about who's keeping score." I let my attention drift, masking my irritation, but it didn't help; the ache under my scar pulsed harder, as if my body braced for the next blow.

Luc glanced up, no doubt sensing the static tension in the room. He'd always been the master at reading the shifts of my mood, like a hellhound for latent violence. "Let it go," his voice quiet but edged. "If you show him it gets to you, he's already won."

I exhaled, "I'd show him a lot more if this curse didn't keep tying my hands." I flexed my left hand, feeling the phantom burn of the scar Yahweh carved into my flesh. Every angel on Earth bore a version of his mark after he lost his own spirit-mate. "He's not posturing; he wants me out before the trial ends."

Luc set down his cup. "Watch your back. With Diablo prodding him, Samael plays dirty." He grabbed his jacket. "Later."

The ache in my chest widened into a scorch. In two hours, I'd stand before a human jury, facing trial seven. Defeat wasn't an option. I scooped up my briefcase and keys, slung on my jacket, and strode out.

* * * *

My office reeked of paper and stale coffee. Ron, the guard, gave a quick salute as I climbed into the elevator. On the fourth floor, the assistant nudged me toward my desk. A tabby cat slinked by, waving its tail.

I rummaged through the paperwork until fingers closed around my Vogel crystal, a pale quartz etched with rune-like veins. It thrummed against my palm, absorbing friction and keeping my angelic energy in check. I slipped it into my pocket, grabbed the outline for today's hearing, and headed for the underground garage. With a two-hour drive ahead; Pasadena to Orange County in rush hour meant careful timing.

Freeway lights blurred past. In my mind's eye, I rehearsed the court-room dance, how to unravel Samael's inescapable charm and paint my client, Jacobson, as innocent. My crystal pulsed, clearing my aura of doubt and calming my system.

At the courthouse, I joined the slow shuffle through metal detec-tors. A pixie's lavender spark winked at me beyond the security line. She outlined a heart with tiny fingers, scenting the air with honeysuckle, then vanished. My mother's voice, soft and distant, urged me not to lose sight of why I fought.

Inside Courtroom Ten, Jacobson sat stiff in his sports jacket, eyes hollow with dread. His wife and daughter bowed their heads like wilted flowers. I clasped his hand. His flesh was warm, trembling.

I clenched my Vogel crystal, my fingers lingering there a moment too long. It vibrated against my skin, throwing off his fear, but not mine. "Relax, I'll prove your innocence." The words sounded hollow in my own ears.

He swallowed hard. "Save my family."

"You deserves justice and today it will happen." I hoped, hearing Samael's mocking voice still in my mind.

Above the camera rig, Archangel Mikael hovered, a silent sentinel. His wings were folded arms of iron.

When the prosecutor's barbed words about "ultra-affluent manipu-lation" dripped through the courtroom, I let them settle before stand-ing. My suit jacket felt like battle armor. I caught each juror's gaze: tired teacher, day-laborer, mother with worry lines.

"My client," I began, voice even as a blade's edge, "is the one who got framed." I sketched a scene of boardroom betrayal. "He fought big corporate power, not the poor he championed." I paused, letting the silence bloom. "Does this man deserve to lose his family for a crime he didn't commit?" I felt Jacobson's hope kindle.

A hush settled so deep I heard the soft click of pens. Mikael shook his head in warning.

Lunch recess came too soon. As I left, Mrs. Jacobson's shoulders slumped; her aura flickered pale. The teenage daughter's glare burned with unspoken anger. I slipped a reassuring nod to security guard Kevin, then crossed the street to my usual corner booth at the cafe.

Shelly slid an iced tea toward me. "Rough morning?"

"Depends on your definition." I juggled memories of the courtroom.

My brother Gabriel appeared, grin shining. "Lunchtime guard duty?"

I dropped into the seat opposite him. "Jacobson's fate is stuck between the devil and the deity."

Gabriel leaned forward, voice low. "Lilith has Samael by the balls."

I braced myself. "Not another wager."

"She'll withhold herself for ten years if he loses again."

A hollow ache hollowed me further. So, this trial wasn't just about justice. It was Lilith's cruel game, testing a man's faith for amusement. "He dies in the underworld if he fails."

Gabriel's face darkened. "Yahweh ordained it. Free will trial."

I slammed my palm on the table. Fries skittered. "I won't accept that."

Shelly intervened, whisking away plates before we drew more attention. I took a deep breath. "I'll finish the paperwork at the office."

Gabriel placed a twenty on the table. "Council of Sarim convenes at sunset. Yahweh demands your presence in Kumuria."

"A meeting during trial? Not negotiable." My jaw clenched.

He stood, shoulders squared. "No choice."

I let him go, the weight of divine decree pressing at my throat. Tomorrow the actual battle began. It was where justice, love, and cosmic wagers would collide, and I'd give everything to bend fate toward mercy.

* * * *

I slipped through the roaring crowd to our courtside row. Luc waved me over, nodding at the two redheads already settled in our seats. Only my twin could score L.A.'s sexiest auburns. My pulse quickened.

They rose as I approached.

"Moira, Brigit, this is my brother, Uriel."

Moira stepped forward first, her nails painted deep sapphire, auburn waves catching the lights like embers. She squeezed my hand just a beat too long; her eyes shone with humor.

Brigit looped an arm around Luc. In ripped jeans and scarlet stilettos.

"Courtside. Impressive," Moira murmured, voice soft as cake batter.

I grinned. "Basketball fan?"

"On TV," she laughed, and honeysuckle drifted off her, familiar so I couldn't forget.

"So, what do you two do?"

Brigit raised a brow. "Paranormal investigator, CIA branch."

Luc whistled, eyes roaming over her dragon-and-flame tattoo. "Never guessed."

"And you?" I asked Moira.

"I own Feathery Bakery and Cafe. Our crumb cake's legendary."

"Best in the state."

Luc folded his program. "Cupcakes too."

I glanced at the court. "Odds?"

Moira's eyes shifted to the scoreboard. "Lakers by six, but Washington might sneak a two-point win."

I chuckled. "A loyal fan."

Brigit high-fived her. "I told you that you would like them."

Moira's russet curls framed pale skin; beneath her glamour I sensed gold-and-green light. A nordic signature. "What pantheon?"

She met my gaze. "Seidr of Alfheim."

"I'm a Throne angel of Kumuria," I admitted.

She only smiled. "I know who you are."

A hush fell as the anthem soared in her clear, lyrical voice. Memories of Aurora's song stabbed at me. I closed my eyes, forcing calm.

The game began. I leaned forward as the balls thundered.

Moira nudged me. "Lawyer?"

"White-collar trials." The thought of Jacobson under Lilith's torture shadowed me. "One case worries me."

She stared at me. "Trouble off the court?"

"Always."

Her lips curved. "I'm a light fae."

"Honeysuckle gave you away," I said.

"My best friend, Katrina, has a signature scent."

"Katrina visits the courthouse periodically."

She blinked. "She mentioned you and said we should meet."

I settled back. "Why are you here?"

Brigit's fingers tapped her knee. "We need passage to Tartarus. A demon, Valefor, stole a necromancy grimoire."

I laughed softly. "Tartarus? Angelic law forbids it. Only Luc's key opens any underworld gate."

Luc stiffened, hand brushing the infinity key at his neck.

"We have other value to offer," Moira voice low.

They drifted off toward the concession stand. I watched them go, unsettled.

Moments later, Brigit reappeared, slipping her hand into mine. "Quiet spot?"

I led her down a dim corridor. Neon light glinted on her determined face. "Why Tartarus?"

"Valefor fled to the underworld with the book. If he vanishes through Muspelheim, we lose him and the grimoire." She drew a breath. "Ecne sent us."

My chest tightened. Ecne, old war brother. "Your cousin?"

"He said you'd understand once you accepted the call."

I exhaled. "You need my permission to break angelic law."

"Just permission and a distraction for Lycre's Ravens while we search."

Lycre, Raven leader, another pantheon's enforcer. "You'd force me to betray my oath."

Brigit's eyes flared. "We wouldn't come if it weren't urgent. A Fomorian witch, Carman, will escape Muspelheim without that grimoire."

I pressed my palm against the cold wall. "I can't grant you Tartarus entry."

She stepped back, chin high. "Then we'll find another way."

Her defiance burned brighter than any ember. I turned and left her in the corridor.

Back at my seat, Moira pumped a fist as Lonzo sank a buzzer-beater. "Sweet cheese, I live for that!"

Luc elbowed me. "So? What'd they want?"

I leaned in. "Brigit needs access to Raven territory and Tartarus to trap Valefor. We have to warn Odin and Lycre."

He drained his beer. "Consider it done."

The crowd's roar washed over me. The Lakers led, but my actual game had just begun.

Chapter Two

MOIRA NAETRA

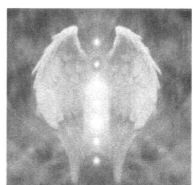

My lungs burned as I crashed through the hardwood trunks, splinters snapping under my boots. The forest's shadows leered at me. Cold shapes slipped through the pines. I skidded over tangled roots and pitched forward. I wrenched at the vines that coiled around my ankles, but the more I struggled they tightened like iron chains.

I gasped and sat upright in my bed, sheets twisted around my waist, my heart hammering so hard I'm sure the walls could hear. The morning sunlight soothed away the last of the dread as the recurring dream faded.

I was safe. I gripped the sheet and fought back the terror of my nightmare. Ever since Valefor disappeared with the ancient book of the dark arts, I'd had horrible dreams. Concern washed over me. A magical war between light and dark factions could create a severe imbalance if the wrong person attained the knowledge of the maps to the magical passageways.

After Velafor took the grimoire, I hid the other two books deep within Nidavellir, home of the dwarves in the Nordic pantheon, for safekeeping. I sniffled and wiped my face with the back of my hand.

Clammy from the dream, I headed to the shower and turned it on as hot as I could stand. I allowed my body to calm as I brought my emotional chaos under control. Turning the water off, I toweled my hair and body. This morning, I'd promised my best friends pancakes.

Looking out the kitchen door into my flower garden, I soaked up the refreshing energy of the early morning, filling my spirit with the positive emotional healing I'd need to weave and practice my spell-casting. A sigh escaped me.

As a Seidr priestess, I would take part in the ancient Nordic ceremony on the first blue moon of the year. This year, Freyr and Freya had chosen me and five others from Mythos Academy to compete for the single position in Freya's superior warrior squad. Being one of Freya's mage warriors took years of training to master fighting skills, along with perfecting the use of magic in battle. They gave the honor to very few graduates of the academy of the supernatural.

Since I was a child, I heard Father's lecture about being one of Freya's mage warriors. Truth be told, I preferred the kitchen. My baked goods carried healing properties that soothed a person's darkest emotions. If someone needed to experience compassion, I'd make them orange vanilla wafers. For love, I'd make strawberry tarts, and for strength, granola spice raisin cookies.

I tapped my fingers on the windowsill. If the books of magic disappeared and someone didn't return them to their chamber at the academy, I would suffer humiliation in front of the entire light elves' court. I'd only unlocked the weave to the books to practice working with the Seidr book of knowledge. Why had Valefor, a friend I'd known since childhood, taken the necromancer text? His theft bothered me unless someone forced him to steal the book.

I closed my eyes and hoped Brigit was successful in using the amnesic potions I created to steal the key from Luc. Last night had been fun, and I regretted having to trick the Connor men, but fate left me little choice. I needed the key to follow Valefor into the celestial underworld, where rumor mentioned that Lilith desired the text.

Flaming hot biscuits. Images surfaced of the Sarim prince, so perfect and yummy with his handsome, milk chocolate skin and his greenish-blue eyes that reminded me of a nest of robin's eggs. If Brigit took the infinity key, any chance of another date with the Connor men flew out the window. We'd be lucky not to face the Throne court on our own thievery charges.

Sunlight filtered through the swag of my country garden curtains. The brisk summer breeze blew in the fresh air. Blue jays sat on the rim of the fountain, chattering to my closest friend, who sunbathed in the birdbath.

Katrina made any pool of water her playground. "We have shower facilities," I said, out the open window.

"And miss out on the gossip of the blue jays?" Katrina's lyrical voice chirped like one lark flying above. In the flowerbed, blue and yellow bonnets danced to the birds' morning song.

"I'll make us a cup of tea." I put on the kettle.

Katrina fluttered her wings and flashed to the herb garden, where she shifted into her human form.

I pulled out a large mixing bowl, a bottle of enhanced knowledge and camouflage potion. If Brigit got the key, we'd have to act fast. We'd need all the luck in the world to find Valefor before the book fell into the wrong hands.

As she entered through the back door, Katrina sang, bringing in a mixture of berries and honeysuckle from the garden.

"I want elderberry cakes. A glorious way to start the day."

"Take a shower, and I'll finish breakfast. Knock on Brigit's door to wake her up."

I poured milk and cracked an egg into the flour mixture, then added the fresh berries. Tapping into my magical ability to connect with emotions, I dashed the mixture with a touch of optimistic hope for our success.

Twenty minutes later, Katrina sat at the table, hair wrapped in a towel, wearing a flowing sky-blue blouse, making her appear more etheric than human. She drizzled berry syrup over her pancakes.

"Do you want any bacon?" Witnessing her wrinkle her nose in disgust was quite enjoyable.

"Two more pancakes, please." I plopped two onto her plate.

Brigit strolled out of her bedroom, hair bedraggled. She pressed the tips of her fingers to her temples and moaned. Wearing a pair of sweats and a sports bra, she sat at the table with her knees pulled to her chest. "I'll take two of those cakes, if you don't mind."

Her tone was a little too grumpy. Had she not succeeded? This was our only hope.

"Coffee." She'd be fine once that first shot of caffeine jolted through her veins. I'd made the pot strong, just the way she liked it.

I smiled at my two best friends. Brigit had a terrifying right hook and a temper that matched her warrior Celtic origins. She constantly stirred up trouble.

Thank God for Katrina, capable of channeling the powers of others. She saved our backsides many times because of her tiny size and soft-spoken, demure quality. The three of us complemented each other. It didn't matter that I'd say a spell and the opposite would happen; then, Freya would test to see if what should happen did. Somehow, my friends would join me and take whatever tongue-lashing I received for not using my gifts. Freya complained I wasn't embracing all my magical powers, and that I was in denial of the real magic within me. Maybe she was right, but then why was I invited to become one of Freya's special mages?

My fingers trembled, and I gripped the fork tighter. I had to learn why Valefor had taken the book. I placed pancakes and bacon on my plate. "When did you get home?"

"Around three." A red-hot glow of happiness radiated around her. She'd either succeeded, or Luc was one super stud.

"Did you get the key from Luc?" Katrina asked through a mouthful of sweet elderberry pancakes.

A triumphant grin sparkled in her eyes. "Success after a wonderful night of sex. I used one of your amnesiac potions after he went to sleep and switched the keys and left him a beautiful tattoo to remember me."

Thank the Fates. "Excellent. Let's hope he doesn't realize he's wearing a replica, not the real carcanet around his neck." Brigit reached into her sweats and pulled out the silver vintage skeleton key with a diamond dangling from the handle. She placed the key in the palm of Katrina's hand.

The diamond's magic vibrated and turned into a light shade of lavender. I bit down on my bottom lip, watching Katrina tap into the stone's power. As the power entered her body, Katrina's aura shimmered in a variegated rainbow of color. Not sure what to do, I pushed back my chair, ready to snatch the object from her hand.

She dropped the pendant and placed both her palms on the table. "Wow!"

"What?" I'd never seen her react like that from touching objects. Katrina was our resident magic stealer. She could tap into an object or person's power and enjoy their strengths for a period.

"This is some powerful shit." Katrina's skin glistened a burnt orange.

"Can you use it?" Brigit asked.

I knew she recognized the firepower oozing from Katrina.

"You bet I can."

"Throw a fireball at me. Last night at the basketball game, Uriel mentioned the fire dragons," Brigit said.

Katrina's eyes narrowed as she drew back a hand and arched her arm forward.

Brigit reached up and caught a torch of light. "This is perfect," she gasped.

"Look!" Katrina held her left arm across the table as a sword and flaming torch took shape on the inside of her forearm. "I could really kick some warrior butt with these." A triumphant smile crossed Katrina's face.

"Be careful." Brigit took the infinity key and placed it around her neck.

I placed a pancake on my plate. "Eat up, ladies. We have to find Valefor before someone causes him harm, or the angels learn we have the key." Failing would not only result in my being humiliated in front of the Seidr coven, but also make becoming a priestess the least of my worries.

* * * *

Uriel

Brassy fanfare exploded from the bathroom radio, Gabriel's calling card. I waggled my ebony wings, spraying water against the stone-tiled walls of my walk-in shower. The hot water eased the ache in my back from the stress of the trial. Either way, win or lose, the competition with Samael would be over.

Using an extra-large towel, I dried my body. My wings receded into my back. Naked, I walked into the closet and put on my favorite gray, twill-woven wool suit. After I covered my sword tattoos, its power surged through my veins. I was ready for a fight.

Luc head appeared in the doorway. His grin widened around a dragon tail ring that looped through his nipple and curled below his jeans' waistband.

"Gabriel's trumpet squeals loud and clear, meaning father wants a word with you, dear brother."

I slipped on a burgundy tie, totally ignoring his last comment. Looking into the mirror, I glared at my shirtless brother and stared, trying not to react to the dragon tail ring hanging from his nipple. He wore the same jeans from the basketball game, and his chain still hung between his pectoral muscles. At least Brigit did not persuade Luc to part with his key.

"Did you score?"

"She's got the best pair of hot lips."

"Too much info, bro." I shook my head and pointed to a gold dragon ring hanging from his left nipple with its long tail wrapped around its body and above his groin, tattooed in red. *Next time!* With *a tiny heart.*

"What the fuck does the witch think she's doing?"

I fought back a chuckle at the dismayed look stamped on my brother's face. "You're a marked man."

Luc's fist came within inches of my nose.

With my warrior reflexes, I stopped the blow and pushed him back against the wall.

"Glad you think this is funny," Luc sputtered, wiping at the mocking red ink.

I laughed even harder. Luc hated being made a fool. "Get dressed." I went into the kitchen and started a pot of coffee. I opened the door and picked up the paper from the front porch, flipping through the pages.

After I wrapped up the Jacobson trial, I'd pay Moira a visit in Sierra Madre and see what I could find out about these mysterious books of magic.

Her elfin image captured my thoughts, and a jolt of desire at the strange animal magnetism surprised me. I hadn't felt such an overwhelming need to mate except for Aurora, my twin soul.

Her internal magic was powerful, but something appeared to hold her back. Doubt registered in my mind about the elfin mage. I poured myself a cup of coffee and sat at the table. Brigit's dragon nipple ring was a definite message, and I meant to learn what those two women hid beneath a veneer of seduction.

Luc followe me into the kitchen and pulled out a frying pan. "Bacon and eggs?"

"Sounds good." I gazed out the patio door, over the cobblestone sidewalk, pondering the missing piece of information.

"You're a thousand miles away." Luc cracked eggs in a bowl and whisked them into the foamy mixture he liked.

"Yesterday, I had lunch with Gabe, and he thinks I will lose, and here's the kicker, Lilith wants Jacobson."

"Shit." Luc put two slices of sourdough in the toaster and poured two glasses of orange juice. He handed me one. "That sucks."

"Lilith loves to find the darkness in men. She'll want to see if she can destroy his virtue and seduce his free will."

"If anyone can bend a man's soul, it's Lilith."

Luc scooped a spoonful of eggs onto his plate and patted the bacon dry. "Jacobson's willing to sacrifice his soul to protect his daughter and wife."

"She'll destroy Jacobson's pure heart just to prove to Yahweh she can."

"He's willing to be a beacon of change. Through his sacrifice, others will benefit."

"At what cost?" Luc sat and ate his breakfast.

"The two-redheads they're hiding something." I sipped my coffee, positive I was overlooking crucial information.

"I was thinking the same thing." He set his fork on his plate.

"Last night, Moira sought the key to enter the underworld. When I refused, I expected her to protest, but she didn't."

Luc reached for his chain. The key was around his neck. "Brigit never mentioned the key, so I had no reason to suspect foul play."

"While I'm in court, pay the ladies a visit. Something is definitely not right. This will give you a chance to rattle their chains and see if they reveal any useful information."

Luc took a gulp of his coffee. "That will be my pleasure. Brigit's got some explaining to do."

"You find the most interesting women." I wolfed down my eggs and bacon. Glancing at my watch, I knew I needed to go. "Text if you learn anything of importance." I grabbed my suit jacket, Vogel crystal, and my briefcase. After tossing my things onto the front seat, I drove the four blocks to the tower building and parked.

Ron, the security guard, opened the glass door. "Thanks."

"Good luck." The security guard, a stout, short man with jolly red cheeks, reminded me of a protective parent watching the tower entrance. I punched the elevator to the fourth floor and the offices of Connor and Connor.

Evelyn cooed at the monstrous tabby cat sitting atop her desk. I swore if I could shift, it would be into a feline. Inside my office, my phone pinged with a text. *Got the information you wanted? I'll meet you in the west parking lot across from the courthouse.*

In the underground garage of our law firm, I tapped the keychain, and the doors of my black BMW unlocked. Traffic on the 57 freeway was relatively light for a Friday morning. I parked at the Santa Ana courthouse.

Joseph, my paralegal assistant, parked beside me and hurried out of his car. Through the window, he handed me a set of files with updated information on two of the jurors. "Good luck, sir."

"Thanks." I skimmed the document, looking for jury tampering. There had to be a reason my brothers felt Samael wouldn't honor the verdict. Nothing. I put the files into my briefcase and headed across the street to the courthouse.

"Hello, Mr. Connor."

Kevin ushered me through the gate. I hurried to the courtroom and took my seat beside my client.

Jacobson gave me an anxious smile. I tapped into his emotional aura and touched Jacobson's shoulder. He flinched. His body was ready to shatter at the slightest provocation.

"Good morning."

"Morning."

The desperation in his tone sounded as if he'd accepted his fate. "I'm confident we've won the case."

"I'm not." Jacobson turned to the gallery, his shoulders slumped.

The shadow of doubt irritated me. Never had I experienced a client so sure he would lose—especially a client who was innocent. I touched my crystal to balance my aura before I faced the gallery of spectators. The benches were full. People waited in the hallway. Extra security arrived and ushered the overflow to another room. Single file, the jury came in and took their seats.

The judge fixed the lead juror with a expectant look. "Has the jury reached a verdict?"

"We have," the foreman replied, his voice firm.

"*He'll please Lilith,*" Samael's voice blared in my ear. "*She'll enjoy toying with his mind. Such weak humans. She'll make him one of her soldiers.*"

My fingers tightened into a fist at my side. "*Get out of my head.*"

Click-click-click-click. The clock's second hand slowed like a time bomb.

"We, the jury, find John Jacobson guilty on all counts of fraudulent conspiracy." The foreman's voice reverberated throughout the courtroom.

The collective gasp startled me. I turned to the gallery in utter disbelief. I shot up. "Your honor, I request a poll of the jury."

The bailiff called each name. One by one, they answered. I sifted each answer and tested it for truth. Ten minds rang pure; two showed foreign threads of dark tendrils, revealing demonic interference. This didn't feel like Samael's work but another demonic force that had twisted two of the jurors' thoughts.

I placed a steady hand on Jacobson's shoulder. He looked up at me, hope and fear mingling in his eyes. I swallowed the bitter taste of defeat. "I'm sorry." My voice was tight as steel. Then I turned away, the courtroom haze blurring around me. I had gambled with lives and lost.

Chapter Three

MOIRA NAESATRA

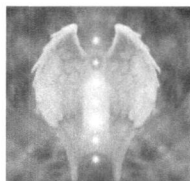

I pressed my palms into the cool dough, fingers working through its springs and coils as the cinnamon swirl took shape. Beyond the bakery's steamed windows, the city's morning rush has thinned to a dull roar. Every knead, every measured swirl of sugar and spice, claws against my racing thoughts. Father will demand my presence at tonight's feast or, worse, march through the realms himself to fetch me. Katrina must smooth his temper, buying us time before Luc and Uriel discover the key's absence. Brigit, Katrina, and I settled on a story we'd use—that I'm off at a sparring match and would return within the week.

Freyr always trained me like a sword-slash of a warrior priestess. Yet he could never fathom my life among mortals in Midgard. To him, blood ties to the pantheon mattered more than the thrum of human heartbeats. I tied my fate to this clan, and soon enough I'd learn my true destiny. For now, Brigit's hunt for Valefor must succeed.

The bell above the door jingles. Luc steps in, shoulders hunched like a coiled viper. I wipe flour from my palms and force a smile. "Coffee? A pastry?" My voice might as well be smoke.

He glared at me and strode past the counter. "Later."

I follow, footsteps soft on tile, curiosity igniting. Out back, Brigit kneels inside a triangle of three slate stones. Between them, the length of Valefor's pale owl feather scarf and the milky quartz I ground into this morning's locator potion glowed faintly. Energy seeps from the stones into the fabric. Now that we hold the key, tracing him should be effortless.

A dry cough out of the corner catches both their attention. Brigit's eyes skewer him with cool amusement. "Luc."

He folds his arms. "Where's your friend?"

"She's across the way." Brigit leans back, letting the warm lantern light sharpen her copper hair. "Care for one of Moira's cakes while we chat?"

Luc's jaw tenses. Brigit licks her lips, then stands, hips swaying like a flame. "Last night was enlightening. Are you asking me out again?"

He swallows, voice lower. "Explain yourself."

Brigit drifts closer. Light shimmers around her fingertips and unlocks a flush in Luc's cheeks. He strips off his T-shirt, revealing the sweep of muscles on his back. When he turns, I bite back a laugh because across his lower ribs, scorched in tiny runes, are the words Next time. And on his left nipple, a slender dragon-ring piercing gleams. This was surely Brigit's handiwork.

Luc's eyes burn. "You branded me?"

Brigit brushes her finger across the scarlet letters. "Men who fall asleep first deserve a reminder of who holds the flame." Her tone sizzles. "You were magnificent."

He's halfway entranced before Brigit shoves him gently toward the bakery door. "Back inside, love. I have pressing business."

I slip in through the kitchen hatch, hands trembling as I check the clock. Brigit will slip to the Raven shifters soon. Katrina's word placed Valefor in their woods. Uriel's doubts already stir; last night he fled from my doorstep like I carried pestilence.

Luc follows her in moments later, tugging on his shirt. I offer him a bakery box. "For Uriel. I tucked in a crumb cake he mentioned."

His scowl softens. "Thanks. He's buried in trial prep. He definitely could use chocolate."

Brigit presses a kiss to his mouth. "See you tomorrow."

Even as the door thuds shut, I can feel the tension drain from her shoulders. She gathers the key's small leather pouch, a vial of truth serum, fresh linens, and trail nuts.

I strapped her satchel onto her waist. "Let's get that book back."

Brigit's eyes flash with determination. "I'll return the key before he senses the pendant's just an illusion."

I exhaled, bracing myself. "May the fates be with us."

* * * *

Uriel

I sank into the battered wooden chair in O'Mally's tavern, its sticky surface barely registering beneath me. The happy-hour laughter swirled like the scent of roasted pine nuts around my head, but I felt miles away. I nursed my third Scotch shot, ice long since melted, and stared at the amber swirl. Samael had outwitted every move I'd laid. I slammed the glass down, heedless of the tiny crack that popped the rim. No amount of liquor would numb the sting of betrayal.

Luc slid onto the empty chair, straddling it so his arms draped over the backrest. His dark eyes reflected the flickering lantern light. "The angels are bored," I growled, voice rough. "They stir up chaos like children with toys."

He waved at the server for two more shots and glasses of water. "Get over it. Dominion wants answers. You skipped the Council meeting."

My teeth ground. "Their blind worship disgusts me."

"Caution, bro. Samael's mated with Lilith now. He'll twist loyalties to please her."

I recalled Mikael's words in the courtroom. Samael had poisoned the jurors' minds. My chest tightened at the injustice. An innocent man lay broken because I'd thought Samael incapable of treachery. I raked a hand through my hair. "If Jacobson keeps his faith, he might still earn Elysium."

Luc drank. "What'll you do?"

"I'll petition the Throne angels for an investigation." I glared at the tavern's dancers, craving solitude.

He shrugged. "They expect you to obey orders. Your attitude's going to bite you."

The sound that escaped me was a low, guttural snarl. "I lost. I failed him." Guilt churned through my veins.

"Fate played its hand. It wasn't just you." Luc clinked his glass against mine.

"I hate it." My eyes focused on the swirling liquid.

"Brothers win and, on rare occasions, lose." He paused. "Now, there's a bigger game. A cosmic poker match for rulership of the next millennium."

My heartbeat thundered. "What?"

"A reunion with our archeia." Luc's voice dropped to a whisper.

Memory exploded in my mind: Aurora's golden hair, her last scream as Yahweh tore her from me. My chest constricted. I inhaled sharply. "No."

Luc laid a hand on my shoulder. "Ecne saved me once. I survived. You can too."

Chamuel swaggered in, then Ananiel, each claiming chairs and elbowing grins. Glasses clinked as they toasted love, sex, and the kundalini dragon's awakening. Rafael traced the scar beneath his heart. Excitement glittered in his eyes; I felt only icy dread. Each brother brimmed with hope. I felt nothing but the icy burn of old wounds.

Luc leaned close. "Meet me on the patio." He jerked a thumb toward the door.

I rose and stumbled past the dance floor into the night's cool air.

* * * *

The tesseract shivered around us, and we landed barefoot on the soft grass of Kumuria. Crystal towers rose like shattered diamonds against the dawn. Zadkiel, sash of purple cinched at his waist, awaited us beneath ivory columns. His golden eyes flared with impatience.

"I apologize for missing the meeting," I snarled, "but Samael's betrayal demanded my attention."

Zadkiel's lips twitched. "Injustice and free will are part of the game. But now, it carries a distinct purpose and a specific assignment.

Luc glanced toward Midgard's distant shimmer. "We're needed?"

"The dark elves have invaded." Zadkiel's voice was calm steel. "Odin begged our aid."

My wing itched, craving flight. "And Brigit?" I asked, remembering Luc's Celtic ring and missing key.

Zadkiel smiled. "Drop the charges against her. Luc, retrieve your key before it's used to unleash old magic. Uriel, yours is to claim your archeia."

My blood chilled. "My archeia?"

He pointed to my beating heart. "Moira holds the Book of Seiðr—its cover embeds the red jasper citrine, a kundalini gem. Only when your spirits meld will it unlock its power."

Luc swore softly. "So Brigit, the key, Valefor's threat, the dark elves are all tied together."

Zadkiel inclined his head. "Odin and Yahweh believe so. Find the book, secure the key, reunite with your mate, and awaken the kundalini within five years—or darkness will swallow the realms."

I pressed a hand to my chest, feeling heat bloom beneath my fingers. Fear and something like longing tangled in my gut.

"Yahweh will see you now." Zadkiel strode away.

We stood under the open sky. Five beams of light pierced the clouds as Yahweh appeared on the lawn, his ebony wings folded behind a purple robe. He raised a hand.

"Reveal your wings." His voice brooked no argument.

Luc's white-pinioned wings unfolded like pure dawn; mine erupted black as starless night. Together, we ascended to his chambers.

Inside, teak cathedrals faced gargoyle statues. Yahweh seated himself as if on a throne carved of light. Luc and I kneeled.

"My sons, humanity teeters in darkness. You must reclaim their other halves to restore balance. The kundalini waits to rise."

Luc's voice trembled. "Why return our archeia now?"

He traced in the air above us. "To understand karmic loss. To heal what was broken." His gaze flicked to me. "Uriel, Moira."

I swallowed. "Her mother is Carman, a Fomorian sorceress. Her father, Freyr, king of the light elves." Mikael appeared with a platter, explaining how Carman had held Freyr in Muspelheim and birthed

26

Moira to claim both magics. The giants' invasion, the stolen necromancy book, the Mare of Nightmares. They all pointed to an apocalyptic alliance unless Moira learned to balance light and shadow.

My ribs ached with wanting and dread. "What must I do?"

"Guide her. Protect her. Let love forge the gem into the kundalini's crown." Zadkiel stood beside Yahweh, certainty shining in his eyes.

Luc clapped me on the shoulder. "Find Brigit, get that key, rescue the book, fall in love."

I stared at my entwined palms and then lifted my eyes to my twin. "Easy," I echoed through clenched teeth.

Yahweh rose. "Feast before the dawn. Tomorrow, Lycre, Odin's raven messenger, will guide you to Midgard."

We followed him into a banquet hall where dancers twirled beneath star-chandeliers. My stomach roiled with apprehension and something like hope. Love had cost me everything once. Now it might cost me more, but without Moira's light, darkness would claim us all.

"The five-year challenge started with the Jacobson trial."

"The dark elves have already declared war within the Nordic pantheon. Therefore, Odin seeks our help." Zadkiel headed for the exit. "Prepare. Together, you and Moira will face your darkest fears. If your love survives, the red jasper citrine will light the way for the resurrection of the kundalini dragon."

"Holy fuck." I wanted to run. In no way did I want this kind of pressure on my shoulders. Losing to Samael and feeling guilty for Jacobson was enough of a burden. No way did I want the lives of my brothers to rest in my hands if I failed to establish the root chakra.

"Are the dark elves and the stealing of the necromancy book connected?" Luc came to stand beside me.

"Odin and Yahweh believe they are."

"What should I do?" Luc asked.

"You must join Brigit, retrieve the key and secure the book. I believe the dark elves will use the Mare of Nightmares to control Valefor."

"Whoa." I flexed my fingers to release the tension building in me.

"Step out to the courtyard. Yahweh will be here in a moment." Zadkiel opened the elevator and headed to the patio.

Five light rays exploded across the blue sky. My flaming sword dropped from above. My clothes evaporated, replaced with my signature breastplate emblazoned with an image of fire. A pair of greaves shielded my lower legs, overlapping my sandaled feet. Vambraces of etched red and gold flames covered my forearms. My royal purple cape hung over the spine of my black wings.

With my full regalia, memories of the angelic war reminded me of what the five lost that day. My complacency coded my veins with ice. I hadn't allowed my light of passion to burn for hundreds of years. "Does Moria know?"

"She denies much of her magic, so I'm unsure of her knowledge. Your archeia grows weak. The impassivity over the centuries blinds her to her destiny. Remind Moira of her beauty and strength. Her mental barriers, much like yours, react with a touch of indifference. To love another, the mirror of alienation must shatter."

Zadkiel's large hand covered the wound over my heart.

"I don't envy you," Luc said.

"What's the plan?" I stuffed my uncertainty aside.

"Find the books, rescue the key, you fall in love with Moira, and locate the gem. Easy!" Luc laughed and reached for my shoulder.

"Right!" I returned the gesture and locked gazes with my twin. Zadkiel stared across the cloudless horizon at the tesseract of dimensions leading to the material realm.

Yahweh joined us in the courtyard.

"Reveal your powerful angelic wings."

Together, Luc and I extended our six wings to their glorious widths. Luc's was radiant pearl white against my own charcoal ebony. Rising high in the air, I flew into the clouds following Yahweh home.

Landing on the lawn, the three of us exited through two marble columns that led into his rooms. Two elegant teak cathedras stood beneath overlooking statues of legendary gargoyles. A silhouetted outline of our mother filled the space.

I hadn't visited this room since the day of the great curse when Yahweh banished Diablo and the fallen angels from Kumuria.

Yahweh sat on his cathedra and turned to me and Luc. "My twin sons, keepers of the gates, we are facing trying times. Much of humanity is shadowed in darkness, and we must balance the scales of justice throughout the pantheons."

Still angry at my father, I crossed my arms over my chest. "Is this why you allowed Samael to break the code of honor of the Throne angels?"

"He'll survive if his faith stays true, especially if the kundalini rises."

"What's your motive? Why are you returning our archeia?" Luc asked.

"Bow down. Luc, you are not a god." Yahweh's voice held no mercy, no passion, as he rose to stand over us both.

Luc kneeled and allowed his wings to cover his head.

"Uriel." My muscles trembled at his tone, and I, too, kneeled on one knee, bowing my head in duty to the creator of our realm.

Now is the time for the kundalini to return. The Sarim princes must gather their mates from around the pantheons and bring forth a new age of enlightenment. Your destiny was always the curse. Do not fail, or the age of darkness will fall upon the realms. Luc, if your brothers succeed, you will bring your mother, my shekina, the Celestial goddess, home."

"Mother has missed you." Zadkiel bowed his head.

"I have wandered empty halls, lost without my mate."

Doing a double take, Luc stared at Father, his expression blanched.

"I have suffered long without her touch."

My resentment eased, seeing the sorrow etched in his eyes. "Why did you make the princes suffer?"

"To understand the role of karmic actions that humans experience. If you were blessed, how could you empathize with people who are experiencing loss?

"Father, you sacrificed your chosen sons." Luc's strained tone revealed the hurt in his own psyche. "I did this for the greater good of humanity."

I turned away, fighting the rise of emotion capable of strangling the air from my lungs.

"Rise and follow me. I will explain the task you and your mate will face."

I extended my wings and followed our father as he traversed over the various spheres of angels busy at their task before returning to the angelic towers. Luc and I entered the common room and met with Mikael.

"A banquet in your honor awaits. Eat before I explain your destiny," Yahweh said.

Mikael ushered us into the dining room and to our places at the table. Zadkeil took his place beside Yahweh, Mikael on the other side. Luc and I sat across from each other.

As the dancers of the court entertained, I could no longer wait for more information. "What can you tell me about Moira?" I smiled at the idea of bedding her, but falling in love wasn't in the cards.

"Half of Moira's power comes from the dark arts. Her mother is Carman, the ancient Fomorian sorceress, and her father, Freyr, leader of the light elves. Carman intends to use her daughter as a vessel to rise out of Muspelheim, home of the fire demons and giants. They will join forces with the dark elves against Freyr." Yahweh took a bite of his roast beef.

"Freyr and Carman?" The pairing of her parents baffled me.

"During the wars of the light and dark elves, the giants captured Freyr and took him to Muspelheim. Carman held him captive and mated with him."

"Holy shit." Luc slicked his hair off his forehead.

"Moira will need your guidance to defeat Carman. She must come to terms with both sides of her magic—the light and the dark."

My heart disengaged and felt like it stopped beating. "What kind of bargain did someone make for Freyr's release?"

"Freyr could take one of his four children. He had to choose between darkness, violence, evil, and destiny. He chose Moira, the chosen destiny."

Everything came together—the kundalini curse and the failure of the trial. These events were all part of the cosmic chess game the gods played. The scar under my left pectoral burned, and I couldn't explain the conflict raging inside. "What happens next?"

"First, we need to help Brigit find Valefor, and retrieve the grimoire. Lycre, the raven leader, and Odin's messengers, will contact you in the morning." Zadkiel paused. "Stay close to Moira; she's vulnerable." As I realized the assignment before me, my anger slowed to a simmer instead of a boiling rage. Father always rolled the deck of cards, and I never knew when the joker was at the top. The seriousness of the situation actually calmed me.

I looked into Zadkiel's strong, determined face. "Can we achieve the unification of the kundalini?"

"I hope so."

Chapter Four

URIEL

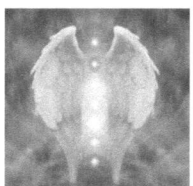

The next morning, I stepped into the office's quiet hum and saw Luc sitting behind his desk. I set his favorite cappuccino on his blotter, then angled my chair toward the balcony's slate-gray sky. My mind drifted to the raven shifters and their unbreakable fealty to Odin, Allfather of the Aesir.

Tap ... tap-tap ...

Three great black birds wheeled in mid–air and solidified into humanoid forms. Lycre, their leader, matched my six-foot-four frame. His onyx eyes glittered, every feather along his broad shoulders ruffled as if bristling with quiet alertness.

Behind him, Hugin stalked forward dressed with a Viking bowman from spine to braid. Munin followed, her lithe form draped in sapphire silk, pupils like twin black pearls. Odin's messengers alone slipped between pantheons, gathering secrets no other shifter could reach. With their aid, finding Valefor and shadowing the dark elves suddenly seemed workable.

Luc bit his lip. "Any word from Brigit?"

I leaned forward. "She agreed to pose as a spell-collector, searching for rare artifacts. Glamor cloaks her identity, in case Valefor's under someone else's sway."

Munin settled on Luc's desk, crossing one leg at a perfect angle. Leather hugged her calf, knives glinting at her thigh. My pulse hitched, reminding me of Moira threading the ball down court. My mate was a paradox: baker by day, blade-dancer by necessity.

"She's got Underworld connections," Hugin said, hefting a massive drinking horn he'd conjured.

Luc scowled. "Valefor's loyalty to the light elves makes no sense unless a demon's puppeteering him."

Munin's lips curved into a teasing smirk. "Surely you didn't miss that our fire goddess wears your key."

Luc's cheeks flamed. I fought a grin. "She borrowed it."

All three ravens exchanged knowing glances and let out a triumphant caw.

"I'd stake next week's salary that Luc thinks Brigit's a catch."

He shot a glare at me. "Is Moira capable in a scrap?"

"Deadly," Munin answered without hesitation. "Her knives flash faster than lightning."

I liked my mate safe and sweet, especially if she kept baking those fudge brownies. But a fighter? I could live with that. "At least she'll survive."

The ravens rose in a synchronous chorus, as if the world itself sighed in portent. Lycre's velvet voice cut through the rippling tension. "Stay in our realm. I'll shelter Moira, track the dark elves, and learn Carman's designs on her. Freyr's been warned that Hagmer gathers forces in the east."

He spun into the leather swivel chair. I handed him my phone. "Add your number."

"Bring the Seidr witch to my manor via the human road—101 Freeway. I'll send Hugin and Munin through the otherworld doors to monitor Brigit's progress."

With that, the three shifted back into ravens and soared into the ashen morning sky.

I turned to Luc. "Find out why Valefor stole only the necromancy text, not the map of the ley lines volume."

He nodded, fingers already tapping on his own phone. "I'll visit the duke's legions, then fly to Alfheim's academy."

"Good. And get that key back before your little spitfire lands in real danger."

Luc's eyes softened as we touched minds, an angelic bond of uncertainty, hope, and that spark of longing. I wrapped him in a quick, fierce embrace. I'd protect my twin with every wing I had. But I needed Moira's heart in return or this whole venture would crumble.

"Courtroom rules, but with swords," Luc cracked a grin.

"Me too."

"Go fetch Moira. I'll meet you at Lycre's in Ventura."

I squeezed Luc's shoulder. "Do you think Brigit's your mate?"

He smirked and motioned toward his own chest. "Spirit-mate, yes. I adore her fire-dragon spirit."

"Crazy bastard."

"The ride will be fun. Now go. Dark elves await, and your sweet baker."

* * * *

Mid-morning sunlight filtered through the bakery's lace curtains as Moira arranged cinnamon rolls on the display. My heart stumbled when the front bell jingled and Uriel filled the doorway. His jaw, carved from marble, held a dangerous promise; the dark curl of his brows made my pulse drum against my ribs.

I smoothed a stray flour smudge from my apron. He smelled of pine and brimstone, an energy so potent I felt my shield waver under his gaze.

"Where's Brigit?" His voice was calm, but the promise behind it made my stomach knot.

I tilted my chin, fingers pausing mid-whisk. "She's around."

His eyes switched from hazel to fire for a heartbeat and then settled back to steel. He crossed the counter and stood over me, heat rolling off him like a second skin.

A ding from the timer saved me. I slid sideways and lifted a tray of golden rolls, trying to hide my tremor. "Fresh from the oven."

He snarled low in his throat. "I don't care for sweet stuff. Where's Brigit?"

I forced a smile and returned to the kitchen. "She went to Alfheim with Katrina to prepare for the festival."

He stalked after me. The air whispered around us. "I've read about your glamour. Don't lie to me, Moira."

My heart thudded. I spooned cream cheese frosting with shaking hands, memories of Brigit in raven territory swirling like bitter smoke. "She's searching for Valefor," I forced calm into my voice.

He closed the distance so fast I felt his chest against mine. "Then you're part of it."

My breath caught. His eyes blazed again. I yanked open the spice cupboard and grabbed a vial of forget-me potion—the quickest way to shield my mind. Two drops into the frosting. I blinked, hoping he'd taste nothing but sugar.

He took a cinnamon roll, ripped into, and closed his eyes as sweetness met spice. Then he set it aside. "Food won't smooth lies."

He tapped the counter. "Sit."

My legs locked. The mailman wandered in, sat, oblivious. Uriel lifted my chin with a finger. "Now." His voice turned velvet, laced with steel.

I led him to the utility closet, my hidden apothecary. Jars of nightshade, mandrake, and dream-dust peeked from shelves. He found the tainted frosting bottle in an instant.

His smirk made my pulse skim the stratosphere. Before I could step back, he pressed me against the shelves, breath warm at my ear. "You're full of surprises."

My heart pitched with fear and parted with something electric. I forced my voice steady. "If Valefor vanishes into the demon realm, Brigit follows him."

He eased off, letting me breathe again. His thumb brushed my cheek, softer than silk. "I needed to know if I could trust you."

I trembled under that look. His gaze flicked to my lips, then back to my eyes. That tiny ripple of desire ignited in my chest.

"I'll watch you. Close the bakery. Pack an overnight bag. You have one hour."

He skimmed his gaze over the brownies and plucked one from the plate. "If you sting me, I'll hunt you down."

His words should have terrified me. Instead, my belly fluttered. He swung out of the door, threw a leg over a gleaming motorcycle, and roared away.

I stood alone in the hush. The clock ticked. My heart still raced like honeyed light. I locked the apothecary, texted Kim that she'd cover tomorrow, then gathered my concealment potions, smoke bombs, teleport balls, and two daggers, one barbed with poison, the other with paralyzing runes.

Before I left, I penned a note for Uriel, packed his favorite fudge brownies in a bag, and taped it to the door. **Gone to see Father.** Thanks for everything.

Five minutes later, I sprinted to my apartment, changed into soft leggings and a cream tunic, strapped vials and daggers at my hip, and slipped into the gloaming. Dark elves massing for war, missing books to retrieve, a guardian angel drunk on my secrets—yet nothing could stop me now. And somewhere in the pounding of my heart, I wondered if, before the hunt ended, I'd find the courage to trust Uriel with my own.

Chapter Five

MOIRA

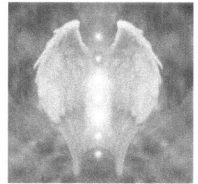

Once I slipped through the ley lines at Hoover Dam, I summoned two glowing runes in the air, sending my shimmer of intent to Dhubagret: meet me in Medalheim's alehouse at dusk. The symbols faded as I climbed into my Honda and pointed east toward the dam's hidden gates into Nidavellir. Forty-five minutes before Uriel realized I'd abandoned the bakery plenty of time to fetch books two and three from my archaeologist friend and slip into Alfheim to speak with Father.

The Taco Bell sign rattled past on I-15; my hamstrings ached from the drive. I parked, unhooked my phone, checked my pouch of potions, and hurried inside. In the restroom mirror, I reinforced my glamour. Dwarf lands were one thing, but secret elfin war plans were another. Hagmer's spies already prodded at Alfheim; I couldn't let these texts fall into the wrong hands.

A teen with tired honey eyes glared as I tossed my paper towel. "Sorry," I offered, but left before she could reply. Back at the counter, I ordered two Taco Supremes.

Number seven, the clerk called.

I found a corner table, tore into the hot sauce packet, and let my thoughts drift to Uriel's fire-kissed gaze. Hormones flared at the memory of his angelic heat, but I rationalized in my mind, no distractions. I finished my meal, checked the time and froze.

My car's trunk lay pried open; two men crouched over it. My breath caught. Hand slipping into my boot, I drew a paralyzing magic blade.

"Go back inside! Call 911!" I shouted to a human couple exiting. The thieves straightened, their eyes widening just as a thunderous roar filled the parking lot.

"What the..."

Uriel roared in on a matte-black motorcycle. He skidded to a halt, kicked up gravel. "Get on!"

I yanked the blade free, two cylinders of fire popped to life on his forearms, and leapt onto his back. The enraged thieves lunged, and he spun a ring of flame around us. Tires bit into gravel; we shot onto the freeway, Uriel's blazing aura whipping wind around us.

Sirens wailed behind. I screamed, "Stop!"

"Not safe," he replied into my mind.

"Stop!" I telepathic screamed into his mind.

"Hang on!"

After miles, he ducked off at a rest area. I slid from the pillion, still gripping my blade. His blue-green gaze held mine, sparking heat through my spine. "Why'd you find me?" I demanded.

He shrugged, amused. "Tracked your body signature."

"You can do that?" Panic rose. My car was my only way to the dam sat abandoned down the highway.

He crossed his arms. "I told you to wait."

"And I told you I didn't need rescuing." Swift as thought, I slashed the air near his throat.

His hand caught my wrist, gentle but firm. "If you want that knife, sheathe it."

I yanked free. "Don't call me deranged."

"Then don't act like a crazy woman."

His smirk danced over the ring tattoos crackling red around his arms. When he flexed, the runes glowed, and a crimson blade bounded into his hand. I stepped back, fascination curbing anger. "Your tattoos burned into Katrina's skin," I murmured.

He sheathed the fire-blade. "Depends on how much magic you borrow." He tilted a brow. "She held power for days."

"She'll need it against the dark elves." I folded my arms, eyes tracing his tight jeans, sculpted form. "Your biker persona suits you."

His grin deepened. "And you like bad boys?" He slipped inches closer, breath warm. I smelled cedar and flame. A moth to his light, I leaned in, his lips hovered near mine. Sparks gathered in his pupils.

For a heartbeat, I thought he'd kiss me. I wanted him to. Then he closed his eyes. When they reopened, the fire was gone.

I scrambled away. "Not really."

He laughed softly and offered me a helmet. "Let's ride."

I resisted, but frustration snapped. "My car."

"Leave it. I'll send someone for it later."

"How can I get my books?"

He tapped the visor. "Brigit's in Ventura. Close the bakery a few days, help her there, then you can meet me at Alfheim tomorrow."

My chest tightened. Brigit should've reached Valefor by now. "Scout's honor, I'll meet you." I held up two fingers.

He kissed the air between us. "Not happening." He dropped the helmet into my hands.

I slid behind him. Instead of north, he turned south. "What are you doing?"

"Heading to Ventura."

"No!" Rage flared. "Stop or I jump."

He laughed into his intercom. "Hope you have magic that prevents roadkill."

I punched him. He only accelerated, weaving through traffic.

By Glen Helen Recreational Park, he finally slowed. I hopped off and bought water and jelly beans, returning to find him straddling the bike. I handed him a bottle.

"Thanks." He twisted the cap. "You okay?"

I hesitated. "They were after something in my car."

"Noted." He pocketed the jelly beans. "Let's talk somewhere safe."

I clambered back on. He twisted onto the off-ramp, weaving past oaks into an open field where campers buzzed by. A banner flapped: Battle of the Bands tonight.

Under a towering tree, he parked beside a picnic table. I removed my helmet and approached. He settled onto the bench, elbows braced.

"Where were you headed?" he asked.

I fingered the water bottle. "The dwarves' gate at Hoover Dam leads to Medalheim. Dhubagret's waiting with the books."

His face gave nothing away. I squared my shoulders. "Uriel, I need to keep them safe."

He cocked a brow. "Hand them to me once you have them."

"No. Odin sent me. Father and I must talk."

He held up a finger. "Keep the Seidr gem safe."

My pulse hammered. "Why do you want the gem?"

He studied me, fingers brushing my hand. Goosebumps rippled. "It's vital, trust me."

My jaw clenched. I took a swallow of water. "Fine. But take me to Hoover Dam now."

He slid from the bike. "Play a game first?"

I blinked as he produced the jelly beans. "Truth or dare?"

I bit back a smile. "What's the wager?"

He flicked a bean into the air and caught it. "Miss, and you answer truthfully. I miss, and I'll do any dare."

I flung a handful skyward. He caught them all without blinking.

I let my glamour drop and his breath hitched. Fair skin tinged rose, pointed ears peeking through russet curls. Fire danced in his pupils again.

"What's up with the flames?" I whispered.

He stepped close. "Do you believe in soul mates?"

My throat tightened. "Why?"

"You're mine."

I laughed, shaky. "You're insane."

He wrapped me in a slow embrace, warmth trailing from his chest to mine. I inhaled cedar and flame, then his lips brushed mine, a weightless touch that set my blood alight. His hands tangled in my hair; for one frantic moment, the world shrank to our heartbeat.

I broke away, chest heaving. "I can't."

He straightened, pulling on his helmet. "Get on. To Hoover Dam."

* * * *

Uriel

I'd argued to return her car on the way back, but pressed the throttle north toward the desert sunset. Years had passed since I'd crossed these crimson mountains; I'd ridden them for pleasure, now worry gnawed at me. Moira's hand occasionally bit at my waist as I leaned through a bend near Fire Canyon Campground.

She pointed to a cliffside cave. "That's our site."

I parked near the visitor center, then maneuvered us down a sandy two-track. At the cave entrance, she slipped inside to find a neatly stashed bedroll and lantern glowing.

"Where'd this come from?" I asked.

"Surprise." She laid out supplies. I watched her strip off her jacket, forearms brushing rock's glow.

She sat beside me. "Dhubagret trades in rare magic. Men will kill for these books."

I shared a brownie and felt temptation coil in my gut.

A soft hiss echoed at the cave mouth. She'd crushed a potion vial. Gray mist curled, petals of night-blooming jasmine swirling in the air.

"Secrecy spell," she explained. "Keeps prying eyes away."

I admired the way moonlight wove through her russet curls. "You're full of tricks."

She shrugged, then grew serious. "I've dreamed of betrayal." Her fingertips brushed my arm. Heat raced through me. Glamour slipped, her brows lifted as she saw the scar puckering across my chest.

I sucked in a ragged breath, memories of divine loss searing my soul. "The angels lost their mates," I whispered. When my mother left Yahweh for banishing Luc and the fallen angels for siding with Diablo, the remaining physical five princes barely survived.

Her eyes glistened. "That's horrible."

"It was cruelty cloaked as punishment. Only by restoring the five kundalini dragon gems that were the hearts of our archeias can we become whole again."

She studied me under lantern's light. "You need the root jasper, the red stone."

I nodded. "It chooses me." I slung my shirt off, revealing tattooed runes that pulsed faintly in the cave's hush. She reached out, trembling.

Our breaths tangled when her lips brushed my chest, then trailed up to mine. The searing heat of the kisses had branded my soul, and I lifted her against the rough stone, my embrace a battleground of doubt and longing. Flames glimmered in my eyes as I tasted her.

She pulled back, fear etched in her eyes. "Uriel…"

"Shh." I cupped her face. "I'm here."

Outside, the night wind whispered through desert sage. In that hush, half-divine and half-elf drew close, two souls longing to be whole.

Chapter Six

MOIRA

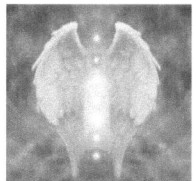

Warm arms wrapped around my waist, and I'd nestled my cheek into Uriel's chest as his curly hair tickled my nose. When I woke, the firelight danced over the dark shadow on his chin, making him look even more mysterious. My heart thudded, and I untangled his arm, sliding back to the edge of the boulder.

Outside, the runic barrier still glowed at the cave's mouth. I traced a finger through the air, conjuring the message I'd sent Dhubagret the night before. No reply yet. I drew another rune, sealed it with my mark, and let it hover until it slipped through the veil. Then I bent to stir the coffee over the embers.

I hadn't heard him approach until his presence heated my back. When I straightened, he stood so near I could count the freckles on his shoulders. His black hair, tousled and wild, made my pulse stutter. "Coffee?" I offered, voice low.

He took the steaming cup without breaking eye contact. The way his throat flexed when he swallowed sent a shiver down my spine. "Thanks." He settled onto a stone, crossing one long leg over the other. "How did you sleep?"

"Perfectly." He rose like a panther, every inch the lethal combination of dark and handsome. Desire flared through me so hot I almost burned.

I carried my cup deeper into the cave. "Still nothing from Dhubagret."

"What now?"

I sketched two lines and an X. The rune glowed gold before I signed it. "I told her we'd meet at the Murky Chainmail within the hour."

He whistled softly. "Impressive. Lost arts."

His praise warmed me more than the fire. "Runic messages are like wordless texts. Seidr sorcerers learned them centuries ago, and today archeologists use them to contact otherworld portals."

Ten minutes later, a pair of icy-blue runes hovered at the entrance. My skin prickled. Dhubagret warned of danger inside Medalheim's gates. I closed my eyes against the chill. "She warns we must be cautious. She'll explain once we arrive."

Uriel's brow rose. "Maybe we wait for more info?"

I jammed my boots on. "We can't. Those books are too important, and she might need help." My hand shook as I tucked my knives away. "The portal's behind that boulder. Take my hand."

His fingers closed over mine. A violet flash winked us through. We emerged behind a wooden shed draped in moss, my usual stash spot. The city's runic sconces cast long shadows on petrified trees.

We skirted the crowded street toward Dhubagret's shop. Merchants hawked wares, but an uneasy hush trailed us. Uriel pressed a finger to my lips as two men in furs lounged outside the tavern ahead. Their conversation came as murmurs.

I wove a focusing charm. Animal paws scurried through the stones, but Uriel tightened my arm and the world fell silent. "Bounty on you," I whispered when words floated clear. "They think you work for Freya."

He drew his sword casually, the steel gleaming. "You'll need a glamour. They'd recognize your elfin features in an instant."

Heat curled along my spine. I willed my hair silver-blond and my eyes sky-blue, cinched into a warrior's tunic. He braided his beard into three thick plaits, the perfect Viking guise.

Inside, the tavern reeked of roast boar and spiced stew. Uriel claimed a spot by a band of djinn and leopards, speaking Norse so flawlessly the bartender nodded in respect. I slid beside him, heart galloping, scanning every table.

A dwarf group in the back eyed us. I fidgeted, tapping the bench in a steady rhythm. Uriel rested his hand over mine. "Relax."

My gaze caught the notice on the door: ten-thousand krona for my head. I palmed my satchel's phone and dialed Dhubagret, straight to voicemail.

Uriel studied me, concerned. "Can you find the books quietly?"

I nodded. "She hid them in an artifact. I just need to trace the weaves."

The bartender lingered at our table, brow furrowed. Uriel smiled and dropped our order: ales and bowls of stew. When the dwarf finally asked where we hailed from, he said, "Muspelheim seeking a magical iron sword."

I leaned in. "Do you know Ganmomri Silvercrest?"

The dwarf's eyes lit. "On the edge of town. Just follow the right coins."

We finished quickly and slipped into a side alley. My fingers trembled as I sent an Elhaz rune to Dhubagret. Books at Silvercrest's.

The alley ahead brimmed with weapon shops and anvils blazing red. Silvercrest himself hammered steel, sparks flying. Hearing my step, he dropped his tongs and swept me into a fierce hug.

"He's safe," he murmured in my ear.

His nose always betrayed me through glamours. I introduced Uriel. Silvercrest grinned. "A handsome Viking."

I smirked at Uriel's growl of possessive pride.

In the back, he presented me with a slim transformation blade, its metal humming. "For the witch who hunts you."

I tested its balance—perfect. "Thank you."

He dipped the blade in magic mist, a ribbon of color coiling into the steel. When the witch and necromancers attacked Dhubagret last night, they stole one book of maps. The other, Dhubagret, had sent to Odin's Norns in Aokigahara.

My knees buckled. Uriel caught me, his arms solid. "You okay?"

I couldn't speak. My future, my life, hinged on a prophecy I barely understood. Silvercrest sealed the blade with a spell. It would shift shape only in genuine danger, but the cost of magic was debt. He shoved us through the back door.

Outside, two goblin soldiers leveled pistols. I yanked a teleport ball from my pouch and smashed it. A swirl of mist ejected us back into the cave.

Our helmets clattered as we sprinted for the entrance. I whispered a forget-me charm behind us, sealing the cave.

When the rumble of Uriel's bike faded into the night, relief poured through me. "Where now?"

"To Ventura," he said, pulling goggles down.

I slid off at my house. "No, you must help me get to Alfheim. My father needs me."

He turned, jaw set. "I need you here."

"I'll go alone if I must." My voice cracked.

He pressed his fingers to my cheek, that familiar warmth igniting me. "Stay one night. Check on Brigit. Then we go together."

I let his hand rest there, savoring its heat. His nearness pulled at something deep inside. I nodded, though my heart thundered at the promise of more time with him.

Chapter Seven

URIEL

I guided the bike onto Lycre's drive and killed the engine. The gargoyled windows seemed to watch us as pixies spiraled from the portals overhead.

Lycre greeted us with his two massive huskies bounding at his side. "We've trouble in Medalheim. Hugin and Munin need to confirm the intel."

"They're on their way," I said, texting Odin's ravens.

Moira drifted into the garden, inhaling the mint and lavender, her golden aura flashing over the flowers. Even here, she glowed like the sunrise.

Lycre led us into his rustic kitchen, where he'd set out platters of potato skins and frosty mugs of Viking ale. Moira sighed with relief as she opened a bottle.

"Did you retrieve the texts?" Lycre asked, voice low.

Moira glanced at me. "Yes, Silvercrest helped. One book's with the Norns; the maps are safe."

Two ravens shifted into their human forms in the garden. Hugin, tall and severe, and Munin, whose eyes gleamed with ancient wisdom, stepped inside.

Lycre gestured to us. "Good. Tell us what you learned."

Hugin snorted, setting down his ale. "Hunters swarm the magical cities. Stay in the human realm until we root out the blood necromancers."

"What of Dother and his demon alliance?" I asked.

His face darkened. "He's sacrificed innocents for power. Loki's blood runs cold compared to him."

The huskies moaned in the next room, and Moira kneeled to soothe them. The sight stole my breath—her gentleness with animals, the soft curve of her smile.

Lycre leaned forward. "Moira's title means destiny. The old wars between Celts and Fomorians will flare again if Carman, the witch mother, regains control through her daughter."

Moira stiffened. Her jaw clenched, and I felt her panic reverberate in my chest. I slipped my hand into hers under the table. "Talk to me," I whispered.

Munin's voice rose above the crackle of the hearth. "On the blue moon, Carman will try to invade Moira's spirit as she takes her vows. She must resist the mares—the dream demons that sow doubt."

I brushed hair from Moira's face. "You're stronger than any curse."

Lycre added, "Embrace your full magic, light and dark. Resist, or she'll consume your power."

Moira's frightened gaze met mine. I squeezed her fingers. "We'll face whatever comes together."

Hugin pressed a sunstone pendant into her palm. "If you need us, name us and clasp this."

Moira closed her fingers around the warm gem, her amber eyes shining. The ragged lines of fear on her face softened at our circle of support.

Lycre rose, nodding to Munin and Hugin. "I'll watch Brigit. You and Uriel should rest before the road to Alfheim."

I stood, relief and something far more tender stirring in my chest. Moira was my anchor, and I wouldn't let destiny pull her away. We'd ride toward that blue moon as one.

* * * *

Moira

Uriel rode in the middle lane, wind tugging at his cloak. I clung to his waist, leaning into his warmth as tears slid down my cheeks. A cool breeze whisked them away, but not the storm inside me. I had just learned my mother was Carman, a necromancer, and my father had hidden it. My thoughts felt like a reactor about to melt down.

Uriel's voice crackled in my ear. "You okay?"

I exhaled. "Imagine a nuclear core that can't cool. That's my brain."

He eased around a slow truck. "Tell me what's behind that."

My fingers tightened on his jacket. Raw magic crackled beneath my skin. "If Dother controls my friends, what's stopping him from using me against Freya's warriors?" My pulse thundered; I had to calm down or risk an explosion. I leaned forward, cheek brushing his back. "Can we go home? Bake? Pretend this never happened."

He slowed near the 210 freeway. Moonlight shimmered off one of his six black wings. "You have a ceremony in Sierra Madre?"

My stomach knotted. "I must recite the Kalevala and earn my stave. I haven't even written my epic."

He glanced back. "You'll earn it. You're strong."

Relief warmed me. "Thanks."

He brushed hair behind my ear. Sparks danced where his fingers touched. "I'll be with you."

My heart fluttered. I dared a smile.

At my cottage, he helped me off the bike. His fingers threaded through mine, a current of comfort and something more. Inside, the scent of sage and galingale root filled the air as I gathered ingredients for teleporting balls. His presence, a steady heartbeat at my back.

Then boots crunched gravel. Four rock-trolls emerged, horned silhouettes under the porch light. A hatchet hissed toward my head. I ducked, drew my curving blade, and backed toward the shed, but not fast enough. A horn ripped into my leg. Pain flared.

"Uriel!" I hissed telepathically.

His form shimmered beside me, invisible to trolls. "Keep their leader alive. He holds the answers."

I uncorked a duplicator potion; a green beam sprouted four mirror-images of myself. Confused, the trolls attacked phantoms. I lunged at the actual leader, my blade ripping through tough hide. Black ichor oozed as he staggered back.

Two trolls hurled boulders. I dodged, but my leg buckled. The third slammed into me; his weight knocked the breath out of me. I thrust blindly as jagged pain seared my arm when troll blood burned my skin.

A crimson lasso wrapped around the beast, hoisting him from me. Uriel hovered above, six wings unfurled, golden fire gleaming in his eyes. His ancient linothorax blazed with the threefold plume of pink, blue, and yellow. He raised his sword; flame danced along its rainbow-hued hilt.

"My archeia," he roared.

My breath hitched. Desire and awe coiled in my chest. Blushing, I turned away and slid my blade home.

He bound the last two trolls against an oak. I pressed my hand to my leg, then drew a vial of truth serum. A lemony mist curled around their heads. Their eyes fogged in compliance.

Uriel's voice was steel. "Who sent you?"

The leader's jaw slackened. "Dother."

My heart thundered. "What does she want with me?"

He whimpered. "The Kundalini Gem. She needs its power, the hearts within, to enslave the pantheons."

I bit back a sob. "And my father?"

The troll's gaze switched to Uriel. "She holds him prisoner, mind bound in chains."

Rage coiled inside me. I closed my eyes for a moment. When I opened them, Uriel's hand found mine.

Together we stood under the moonlit oak, warrior and angel entwined. Sparks of magic pulsed where our fingers met. Around us, the world trembled, but we were ready.

Chapter Eight

MOIRA

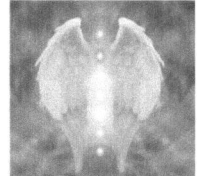

Uriel leaned against the huge sink in the shed.

On the side counter, I finished laying out the herbs that needed to dry and gathered the ones I'd take to my uncle. I'd also have to bring a plate of his favorite desserts. "Have you visited the magical communities here in Sierra Madre?"

"I've used the ley line gateways to reach the elves' territory in Britain. The isles are one of my favorite vacation spots."

"The Celtic lands hold powerful ancient magic, a source of earth power greater than in the Norse realm. I've traveled to the stones for ceremonial worship."

"The call of the stones is in your blood, since you're half Celtic Irish. Does Brigit know of your connection?"

A pang of longing shot through me. I hated being separated from my two best friends. Lycre promised she was safe and watching Valefor. Together, she and the ravens tracked the league of demons following our friend. Apparently, Dother used a mind-altering spell to keep him under his control.

"Let's go to Wildelea, the magical side of town, to talk with my uncle. I need to send a message to my father and warn him of the dangers facing our people." Uriel wrapped his arms around me, bringing me close to his heart. His touch felt like I'd come home.

"I've alerted Luc and Katrina to increase the security around the palace," he whispered into my hair, soothing me with his gentle tone.

His fingers massaged the nape of my neck, making me melt into his warm body.

"I fear Carman uses the dream mares to torment my father in his sleep."

"You must tell your father you know of your mother's identity to allow him a chance to break the chains that bind him to Carman's dark magic."

"I know." I gulped back the sorrow choking my throat. My peaceful life and my relationship changed. I still feared my father's disapproval once he learned of my mistake, giving Carman and my brothers the opportunity to use the grimoire books.

Uriel removed his shirt, and six black wings surrounded my body, immersing me in the brightest light. My anger faded as he helped to level my energy. My mind swam through a haze of feelings, desires, and memories.

"Calmer?"

"Yes, what did you do?"

"I pulled your energy into my body. Before the days of our separation, our two halves always mingled and balanced each other."

The flame danced within his eyes, and I knew he spoke the truth. I'd seen glimpses of a time when we never left each other, a time when we were whole, but now we were both broken.

"I'm gonna take a shower, and then we'll go to Wildelea," Uriel said.

Unable to take my gaze from his V-cut abdomen, I mindlessly handed him a towel from the shed's basin. My legs felt leaden as I moved out the door.

Uriel's hand pulled me to him.

I gasped, needing and wanting this beautiful man. If I didn't leave the room, I'd be jumping his bones and feeling regret in the morning. I left him standing in the doorway as I went to my bedroom and shut the door. The stench of the trolls still lingered on my skin. Stepping out of my clothes, I turned the water to warm and let my stiff muscles relax under the pulsing heat. I visualized Uriel's hands moving over my breasts as I lathered the soap around my hard, taut nipples. Heat curled inside me, threatening my control. My core contracted at the thought of spending the night with him and seeing the burning flame ignite in his eyes. A fire I knew was for me. My body arched, and I allowed the water to tease me while my fingers ended this torture I felt burning inside my hungry soul.

Half an hour later, dressed in jeans, a flowered tunic, and a pair of sexy pumps, I sauntered out of my bedroom and into the living room.

Uriel sat on the couch with an ankle on his opposite knee. He wore another Led Zeppelin t-shirt with a picture of Icarus falling from the sky.

"You know it's the twenty-first century and not 1975?"

"I like Stairway to Heaven. What's wrong with Zeppelin? Anyway, I'm an immortal. What does time mean to me?" He chuckled and sang the lyrics at the top of his lungs.

"You're a strange one. Don't let me forget I need lavender root, tundra safflower, and pinches of mammoth clove."

"No problem."

Uriel reminded me of a golden retriever, all excited to go on an adventure.

"I haven't spent time in the magical city for eons."

"Why not?" I tilted my head and squinted in surprise. "Earlier, you mentioned using the ley lines. Why wouldn't you visit the magical cities?"

"After losing you during the angelic war. I lost interest."

I strummed my fingers across the stubble of his jaw. In waves, I could feel the anguish emanating from him. His pain and loneliness hit me like a boulder to the chest. The impact was like what the loss had done to him.

"You carry tremendous rage inside you."

He turned away from my penetrating gaze and answered my earlier question.

"Since the battle between Diablo and Yahweh, the Throne council prefers the Sarim princes, limiting their interaction with the other pantheons. Our job as Yahweh's angels is to guide humanity. Since the last great celestial battle, that has been our destiny."

He intertwined his hand with mine. "I'd go anywhere to spend time with you, my fair lady." His dark eyebrows arched and rose from the couch. "Lead the way."

I went into the kitchen, packaged muffins, added them to my backpack, and strapped the fanny pack around my waist.

The portal opening paralleled Sierra Madra, right behind my house. Within the magical community, it was a ten-minute walk to my uncle's shop.

"Here we are. Trinkets and Herbs." Bells chimed when we entered, much the same way as in my bakery. The chiming of bells created positive vibes in any room, making people want to savor the wares and spend money. "Uncle Gander, it's me."

My uncle was helping customers, but he waved. "I'll be there in a moment."

Uriel scanned the shelves before he picked up a book, How to Identify and Speak with your Guardian Angel. Seeing the amusement in his eyes, I laughed.

"Should I buy this for you?" He winked. "Looks like your typical New Age shop."

"The store's profitable." I loved coming here. Old magic lived in many trinkets Gander purchased for his human customers, people who dabbled with spells and ritual ceremonies. In the rear, an apothecary housed magical potions I made. Their sales gave me extra income. Uriel thumbed through the various shelves of books. "He carries an assorted selection aimed at the average magic user, with an emphasis on glyphs, artifacts, and symbolic jewels."

"Interesting."

"Moira." My uncle ushered the customers out the door, locked it, and turned on the sign that said I'll be back in fifteen. "My clerk's on his break. When he returns, we'll go into my living area for tea."

Worry creased the corners of his eyes; his movements were antsy and on edge.

"Uriel, this is my favorite uncle, Gander. The smartest elf in all of Alfheim."

"She exaggerates."

Gander's flowered, button-down shirts reminded me of gardens, always filled with cheer and a welcoming smile, but now his green eyes darkened, and the corner of his full mouth twitched.

Uriel extended his right hand. "Nice to meet you."

"We don't see too many angels in our community." He chewed the corner of his mouth while giving Uriel a scrutinizing glare.

What was wrong? My uncle's vibes startled me.

"I met Moira at a basketball game, and I mentioned I'd like to visit a magical city. And here we are."

Uriel took a protective stance close to me. What was up?

"I see."

His tone was disbelieving as he eyed Uriel in the way men do when sizing another man's potential.

"I brought you your favorite chocolate blueberry muffins."

My uncle embraced me. "Need to talk."

At his whisper, I smiled and had to decide whether to include Uriel in our discussion or leave him out in the store. I got the impression my uncle wanted to speak to me alone, but I had no clue how that could happen. "If you have chai tea, I'll take a cup, and then we can talk."

"Give me the list of herbs you need, and my clerk can fill the order."

I handed him the list from inside my fanny pack. "Thanks."

He held my hand and observed the slave ring. "Silvercrest's work. The slave ring's a powerful magical weapon."

My uncle's magical powers spiked when his emotions grew strong, scraping across my shields and causing me to pull my arm free. "Dhubagret's hurt."

There was a tap at the window, and Gander opened the locked door.

Uriel stood behind me with his hand at the base of my back. His heat penetrated through my clothing.

Gander's clerk came inside and took his place behind the register.

"Tomas, watch the store and blend these herbs into one-ounce bags," my uncle said.

My uncle gave Tomas my list. I reached for a few other jars of herbs. "I also need these. My supplies are low."

Tomas took the bags and walked to the barrels of dried herbs. "Will do. Moira, do you need any TP balls?"

"Actually, I do. I'll take all the teleporting balls you have."

My uncle and Tomas both arched an eyebrow.

Gander nodded to Tomas, then he ushered us out the door and to the rear of the building where he lived. Inside, he motioned for Uriel to take a seat in the tiny living space.

Uriel turned around the table chair and sat, placing his elbows across the back.

I moved to the couch, feeling Uriel's intense gaze on me.

My uncle put the teakettle on the stove and sat in his armchair. "What really brings you here today?"

I fumbled with my hands and took in a breath, not sure where to begin. "Last week, Valefor took book one of the sacred grimoires."

"Where is he?" Crossing his legs, he tilted his head, voice oddly calm.

Small splashes of water hit the pool in my uncle's meditative fountain, filling the corner space of the room. He stared, concern in his green eyes. I'd never kept secrets from him. Did my uncle know about my parents? I clenched my jaw, not wanting him to know and not wanting to lose the perfect illusion of my family.

"Brigit tracked his movements between the shifter and human doorways." I avoided mentioning the demon underworld. I didn't plan on letting him know Brigit swiped the key from Uriel's brother and, if the Dominion celestial governance wanted, we could face charges.

"What does he want with the book except to stir up mischief? Have you summoned him?" He asked Moira, but Uriel took over the conversation.

"Brigit's working on it. Lycre, one of Odin's shifters, is positive a Celtic necromancer holds him hostage. Brigit's in Ventura with the ravens, laying out a plan to trap the demon controlling Valefor," Uriel said, drawing Gander's attention.

"Why there?" My uncle leaned toward Uriel and placed his elbows on his knees.

"The locator spell shows him in the area." I moved to the edge of the couch to assert my dominance in a room full of strong male energy.

"If a necromancer confined Valefor to a summoning circle, we're dealing with blood offerings and real dark magic." Gander frowned and ran his fingers through his hair. "He's a trickster, full of mischief but not cruelty."

"I agree."

"Brigit will hold her own against any dark forces." Uriel's confidence calmed my fear. I knew he was right. Brigit could handle fire, and she was a warrior goddess.

A part of me hungered for the knowledge of the necromancers and to feel the dark arts' power in order to understand the hold it held over others.

At Uriel's scowl, I looked away. He'd touched into my thoughts, and his expression tightened with strain. Horror-struck me. I banished those thoughts, fearing the darkness might overtake me like the mares in one's dream.

"Have you discussed Valefor's situation with your father?" Gander asked.

"The grimoire books are my responsibility."

He puffed out his chest in a macho he-man action. "Not if a dark necromancer's involved! Don't follow the elfin demon into the underworld thinking you can recover the book on your own. Blood sacrifices usually carry the power of evil." My uncle looked at me with a stern gaze.

I avoided direct eye contact because that's exactly what Brigit and I planned to do.

Uriel looked from me to Gander and gave a sardonic laugh, sending a direct hit to my stomach.

"Brigit stole the infinity key from Lucifer and plans to follow Valefor. The Throne council has allowed her access to the underworld, against my sound judgment." A note of triumph lingered in his voice.

"That girl has more guts than sense." Gander smiled.

"My brother's still recovering from the special reminder of a dragon ring left hanging on his left nipple."

Uriel tried to keep a straight face but couldn't. His masculine mouth twitched at one end into a wry grin.

Uncle Gander chuckled. "Brigit's trickery is worse than Valefor's. You need to be observant around her."

"What did you want to talk about?" I asked.

"I've heard some disturbing rumors." The kettle whistle blew, and Gander rose. He poured hot water into the teacup before looking at Uriel. "Do you want any coffee?"

"Sure, thank you."

Uncle Gander handed Uriel a cup of coffee, then he leaned against the table. "There is a private family issue that I need to discuss."

"Does it include information about my mother?" I masked the emotions, not wanting to admit the deep betrayal I felt at my father's lies.

"I need to reveal an important secret, something I promised your father never to tell you until after your coronation of Freya's Seidr warriors."

"Don't bother. I already know. Dother, my loving brother, has a bounty out for my arrest." I stood and paced the room, not wanting to deal with the clawing fear seeping into my veins.

"Dother's a violent, disgusting rodent."

A thin smile on his tightened lips and a disturbing change in his tone made me realize that everything about my father and mother was true. I sensed it.

"Today, he sent five trolls to my house. Three killed or incapacitated, and two sent back with a warning." Heat rushed to my cheeks as I dug my nails into the fleshy meat of my palm.

"The books?"

"Dother has the second, and apparently his mother, Carman, wants the third. Dhubagret gave the book to the Norns of fate. It hides in the Aokigahara forest, secured with an unbreakable rune shield."

"Carman is the strongest of the Celtic witches. If she seeks your power, be careful. She is proficient in a wide range of malefic magic and uses a Celtic mare here in the human realm to cause horrific damage."

"How did Carman hurt Freyr?" I asked.

"She kept your father chained in the underworld for three years before he escaped. When he returned from his extended absence, he received protection from Freya. She allowed no one to see him until his strength returned. Someone had subjected him to blood drainage, torture, and revival, repeating the process. No one speaks of those horrid days of mourning."

A burning sensation blurred my vision and was worse than facing Freya after one of my screw-ups. Gander retold the tale as if it had happened to someone else, not my parents. "I've heard none of these stories." I stared at my palms as if they held the reason my mother wanted to harm me. The vision of my parents together kept repeating over and over like a worn-out record.

"I'm here. Lean on me, my kindred spirit. I promise she won't hurt you." Uriel's words soothed my trembling heart.

"Freya told stories of legends to hide the truth of your father's disappearance and to explain your birth. You were an infant, and many rumors flared to life about your true parentage." My uncle reached over and took my hands in his.

My heart hammered in my chest so hard my ribs ached. I choked back the hysteria forming in my mind. "Fudge sticks. I'll need a potent spell. The crazy witch is after me and wants to destroy my family."

"I'd suggest you visit the Norns at the Yggdrasil and consult with the witches of fate. They know of your destiny and how it's related to your mother."

"Asking my father would be easier."

"Whatever way you choose, protect yourself."

Uriel placed a hand on my shoulder. "We should get going."

I reentered the store where three women stood talking with the clerk. My uncle used a warding spell inside the shop, which automatically weakened a fae's glamour shield, so I could identify they were light elves.

Gander reached into a huge drawer behind his counter. "Take the remaining teleporting balls and repellent spells I have in stock."

"Thanks. Saves me the time to make them."

"Be careful. I will inform your father and Freya to reinforce the otherworld and prepare for an invasion from Hagmer. We've expected and prepared for this day. Carman will use Hagmer to carry out her threats." Gander kissed the top of my forehead. "Hurry and stay close to your angel."

I placed the potions and my purchase of herbs into the backpack as two men entered my uncle's establishment.

They touched objects and opened books.

As prickles of alarm raced up my spine, I drew out my knife. I tugged on Uriel's arm and pushed him toward the door. "Bounty hunters!"

My uncle came up to Uriel and slipped a small object into his hand. "A portal stone. Pleasant journey. Now go."

Gander stepped in front of the two men.

In giving us a head start, I didn't know how much time it gave us.

I moved to get outside so as not to trigger a fight inside my uncle's establishment. Leaving the building, I took the three steps onto Kevlar Street and tensed, waiting at Uriel's side for the attack.

"Come on," I yelled as we ran down the cobblestone street, past the local eateries and my favorite candy store. The crossroads were two hundred feet ahead, which led into the City of Sierra Madre. I turned and spotted the two men behind us. A surge of wild panic welled inside me, then two men came from the left, attempting to box us into a trap. A magical complex weave ambushed us on this side of the veil. "Uriel, we're trapped."

"I have a plan."

"Let's hear it, because at the moment, I'm out of ideas."

"Get behind me." Uriel unsheathed his sword, and yellow flames danced all around the blade. Holding my hand, he sliced through the weave of magic blocking us from leaving the city. As a circle of fire erupted in front of me, I screamed.

Uriel dragged me along a raging path of flame.

"Trust me."

One man aimed a pistol at my heart. I would die right here. A slow tremor vibrated through me. I tensed, expecting the arrow's puncture, when Uriel dove in front of me. The bullet pierced his chest as he pushed me through a blazing ring of fire.

"Drop and roll," I heard someone yell. Was I on fire?

Water sprayed across the hillside as firefighters rushed to control the exploding flames. Two paramedics grabbed me, throwing an oxygen mask over my face.

I looked around. Tears formed in my eyes. The portal closed, and Uriel disappeared.

Chapter Nine

MOIRA

Only a couple of hours had passed since the fire and Uriel's disappearance. Sitting in my herb garden, I thought about my father and the strange twist to our lives. I really had to go to the bakery. No way I would sleep tonight, so I might as well work. A shooting star streaked across the black velvet sky overhead, and I closed my eyes and called on Odin for help. Had he escaped the magical realm? I pushed back the tears, refusing to believe he was dead. Not Uriel.

I wanted my two best friends. I needed them to help heal the gaping hole in my heart. Uriel called me his mate, his kindred spirit, and I'd scoffed, not believing his fanciful tale. Losing him tore me to shreds. I'd never accept that he wasn't coming back. He was helping me, but more importantly, he was my lost spirit soul.

Grateful that Uriel's paralegal assistant had retrieved my car, I closed my door and wondered how my roommates were doing. Katrina was still in Alfheim, and Brigit, with the ravens. I found my car parked in the driveway and located the keys under the floor mat. The thought of him returning to my car caused a whole new bucket of tears to gush. Drained of emotions, I slumped over the steering wheel. I couldn't allow the sadness to seep into the baked goods, or hundreds of innocent people would experience my loss.

When I woke up the next day, I was sitting in my car, holding onto the stuffed tiger that always traveled with me. Feeling achy, I dragged myself to the house and took a shower, getting ready for work. I had twenty minutes before the bakery opened but was cutting it close. I called Jill, my go-to girl.

"Hi, sweetie, what's up?"

"I'm running behind. Can you get to the bakery and make sure the night crew's doing okay? I'll be there within the hour."

"No problem. You all right? I heard about the fire out your way."

"Everything's fine. I just stayed up too late."

I couldn't tell her my world was falling apart, and I might be responsible for the death of an angel.

Most of the morning customers had left, and I had a moment to relax. I gazed out the bakery window, enjoying the bright sunlight streaming inside. My thoughts drifted to Uriel, wishing he'd get in touch.

Lycre came up behind me and glanced over my shoulder. "What are you looking at?"

"Can angels die?" I asked, staring toward the San Gabriel forest.

"Trust me, he lives."

I gave him a weak smile, returned behind the counter, and dished up a hot, buttered chocolate muffin for the homeless man sitting on the bus stop bench. "Will you give this to Joe? He's the one sitting in the corner."

He took the muffin and coffee I handed him. "You wouldn't have another of your apple strudels hidden in there?"

"Come back and take a seat at the counter. I'll bring you a cup of coffee and strudel, and you can tell me about your plan."

"Can you be ready to go within the next couple of hours?"

"Sure." He left the bakery.

My stomach curled at the risk we all faced if our calculations of the demon attack were wrong. I popped a cherry tart into my mouth to settle my fears. Instantly, the juice calmed my nerves. Tonight, we'd end this charade and call the necromancer to the surface. And hopefully free Valefor from the confines imprisoning him.

The morning disappeared in a rush of last-minute orders. I barely had time to finish and prepare for the weekend when my afternoon baker came through the door.

"Hey, boss."

Jorge was a slim man for one who worked in a bakery, his dark hair pulled into a ponytail with a fishnet cap. "Hi, Jorge. Sorry about the powdered sugar still glazing the baking vat. I'm finishing the lemon bars."

"Anything I can do?" His kindness calmed the frenzy I felt at finishing up the baking.

"Cookies are in the oven. They should be ready."

"Any special instructions?"

"Our specialty orders are in the rear refrigerator. Call me if any problems arise. I'll be in Ventura until things work out. I'm not sure how long."

"The bakery will survive a couple of weeks without you. You deserve the time off." Jorge took the cloth from my hands and began wiping the counters.

Jill handled the register.

Together, those two were a perfect team, and I knew things would be fine.

Jorge touched my hand, giving me a moment to relax. I released my breath and attempted a smile. Jorge understood my obligations as a magical warrior and kept my secrets whenever I suddenly left. Usually, the assignments for the Mythos Supernatural University were rare, but I was in training to take my place in Freya's special squad.

I washed up and removed my apron. Lycre would return to my house in less than an hour.

"Go."

I wove a protection spell around the bakery. I loved Sierra Madre, the bakery, and my home. If war broke out in the magical world, I might have to sell the bakery and move back to Alfheim. The pantheon councils would surely close the portal entrance into the otherworld realms. If humans became involved, they'd never survive the cruelty of magic forced on their lives.

* * * *

The orange-reddish hues of dusk signaled an ending to the longest day of my life. Sitting in Lycre's kitchen, he and I reviewed the plans to steal back the book.

Hugin and Munin came in through the window and shifted forms. They also wore black attire.

Brigit, dressed in black leggings and a red tank top, took my hand. "You ready, Moria?"

I squeezed her hand, eager to be doing something. My mind barely wrapped around Uriel's disappearance. Lycre continued to encourage me about Uriel's survival and promised he'd return to us as soon as he could. The aching hole in my heart grew by the hour.

"Dother doesn't suspect we know of his plans. It's a perfect opportunity to trap the necromancer and seek the help of the demon world," Lycre paused and looked around the table. "So be cautious of offending them."

The five of us grasped hands, and I dropped the teleporting ball and crushed it under my foot. We arrived at the industrial compound where Brigit had last traced Valefor. A massive corrugated-metal building stood to our left. I cringed at the whine of metal grinding against metal. "Creepy place." I moved closer to Lycre.

"Look at the arrangement of stones surrounding those concrete slabs. Enclosed in the center is the Algol, the mythical gorgon Medusa, the demon's head," Brigit said.

Scattered across the area, I walked over to find the remains of animal sacrifices. Turning away, I fought the bile surging up my throat. I hated ritualistic magic and detested those who offered blood sacrifices in trade for favors. Valefor was not a lower-level entity, but a duke with his own legions of demons. We had to find the book and release him from their grip before they killed him.

Shadows crept between the buildings marked with demonic crosses and Algol symbols. This place was downright spooky, and I couldn't control the heebie-jeebies creeping along my neck and making every strand of hair stand at attention.

"Go to the right." Lycre pointed toward Brigit and me. He went to the left, and two ravens flew overhead.

Brigit took the lead.

I stayed a couple of feet behind her.

Two men in leather pants with a chained pouch connected to the belt loop emerged from a small door at the rear of the building. The one on the left raised his hand above his eyes, searching the property.

Brigit and I halted, waiting to see what his next move would be.

I leaned over and edged my hand into my boot and pulled out my blade laced with poison.

Brigit reached behind her back and signaled for me to get out of the way.

She was about to set this place on fire. "Wait," I hissed. "You can't burn the area like a fried egg, or we'll all go up in flames."

One man was Baal, the demon of war. I recognized him now. He wasn't shielding his appearance anymore, with his goat-like head and owl wings protruding from his upper back.

The other man's handsome face resembled my own. I drew back in surprise and fought the desire to call out to him.

With the spell book open, he called out, "Extiegris Annoiato," Dother bellowed.

A hundred feet in front of me, the ground opened, the air grew heavy with the weight of sulfur. A clear emerald light flashed, and several particles shot out from the terrain, forming into spectral demons.

Lycre shifted. His raven form joined Hugin and Munin in battle with the creatures.

"Hot fudge." I jabbed my knife into the belly of the nearest creature. It had no effect. Since they were phantom demons, traditional weapons couldn't kill them, so the little bastards just kept coming and puncturing my skin.

Baal opened a gateway, and he and Dother disappeared with the book.

"Go after them," I yelled to Brigit.

With Lucifer's key, Brigit jumped through the shimmering, ebony-gray portal.

I fought two spectral demons, who focused on the slave ring attached to my middle finger and wrist. One creature gouged its sharp fangs into my arm. Blood sprayed through the air in a fine crimson mist.

As his fangs released their hold, I jerked my arm close to my chest and groaned as the air hit the wound.

A murder of ravens appeared and attacked like a well-trained militia, but had little hope of defeating a foe they couldn't kill.

"Go," Lycre said.

The shimmer of the portal was fading. As I realized my best friend and the grimoire had disappeared within the underworld, an icy shiver of apprehension made a slow crawl up my spine. With a powerful force of momentum, I dove through the portal before it closed.

Baal and Dother disappeared around the bend. I expected to see brimstone and fire. Instead, a desert cavern with boulders, water, and dirt.

"You okay?" I asked Brigit, scrubbing bits and pieces of rock from the palms of my hands.

"Just a couple of gravel burns. You?" Brigit sat on a large boulder, wiping her knees.

"I'm bleeding from my thigh. Holy fudge, it hurts." Without warning, my body grew limp, and lights danced in front of me as I staggered and went down hard.

Brigit took my wrist in her hands. "Your pulse is through the roof." Her eyes scanned my body and stopped at a rip in my leggings. A fang protruded from my right thigh. Brigit ran a hand down my leg and examined the wound. "This is severe."

"I gotta pull out the fang." Brigit removed her blade and gave me the sheath to put between my teeth.

"Use your knife to cauterize the skin, or I might bleed to death." My words were weak.

Brigit placed the metal in her palm and sent fire to heat the blade.

Using a calming spell, I closed my eyes and sent a message to my nerve centers. I didn't know if it helped, but the bleeding had to stop before I passed out. "I'm ready."

The anguish in Brigit's eyes reflected my revulsion at watching my flesh sizzle.

"Chocolate kisses and gingerbread houses, that fucking hurts," I muttered.

Brigit laughed. "If this were me, I'd sound like a sailor after a hard night out."

Two burned patches stopped the flow of blood. At least, I'd live to see another day.

Along the sandstone walls, tiny creatures with vicious eyes stared as strange sparkles escaped from their meager mouths. I cringed at the horrible sounds the ugly things made.

"What are they?" Brigit backed toward the opposite wall.

"Nothing I've ever encountered."

"We need to get out of here."

Uncertain about which of my potions would work against these creatures. "I'm not leaving without the book."

"That's exactly what I expected you to say. Brigit created a path of fire between us and the creatures. Like a piece of fresh steak, they stared at us. Up the wall, they skittered around the fire and straight towards us. "They're not afraid."

I reached inside my boot and retrieved another knife I'd laced with an immobilizing potion. I tossed the blade to Brigit. "It won't kill, but it'll incapacitate them long enough for us to get out of here."

"On three, aim for the eyes." Brigit dashed toward a group clustered together. "Three!"

Holy moly, these creatures darted out of the way so fast that I had little opportunity to wound any of them. "We really could use Katrina right about now."

"You aren't kidding."

One creature flew in and out of the fire with no adverse effect.

"Cast a disappearance spell," Brigit muttered as they surrounded us.

I squared my shoulders against her back and intertwined my fingers with hers in reassurance. "Ready?" I unclasped my hand and opened my palms to visualize a location. As I stretched my wrist, I gritted my teeth and fought the burn coursing through my arm.

"Will you hurry?"

"I am light. Return to the dark where shadows dwell."

"Hold on."

Brigit said before we both landed in an underground cavern. "What happened?"

"You sent us away instead of those demon leeches."

"That works" I followed the passageway down to a river. The rancid odor of decaying animals and rotting vegetation stung my nostrils and assaulted my senses.

"Where do you think we are?"

"Smells like a swamp."

"Swamps usually mean snakes and slimy critters." A displeased scowl dipped Brigit's brow lower, and she gave an exasperated sigh. "What do you want me to do?"

A cloud of gnats hovered in the air, driving me crazy. The slurping sound of mud burbling and the musty smell of damp earth rose to violate my nose. This was no place I wanted to stay. "We've got to get out of here."

"How?" Her eyes narrowed, and Brigit's snarl now turned into an outright frown.

Her look of disgust said this was all my fault. She knew that most of my spells worked in opposition to what I intended when I got nervous, so she shouldn't be angry. "I'll use the same chant."

"Let's not! I'd rather look for a way out of the tunnel through a door and not risk the uncertainty of you casting another disappearance spell." The luminous motes floating in the murky water were our only source of light.

"Search for a doorway or portal to the surface." I walked along the swampy shore that lined a river of mud.

Up ahead, a turtle's shell parted the duckweed as it swam through the murky water.

My imagination conjured many creepy critters. Not much scared me, but I really hated bugs that crawled in dark places. Struggling to concentrate, I searched for the magical signature of a doorway to identify where we were. The reek of swamp leaves interfered, making smelling or seeing any magical sparks difficult.

The landscape hadn't changed for the last mile, just a river of mud and species I'd rather avoid. "Do you sense any magic?"

"Not yet. The humidity's like a steam bath." I wiped a sweaty arm across my forehead, but it didn't help.

"Do you hear a rustling noise?"

I stopped. Listening, I sensed a wise creature, one who carried knowledge of the cycles of change. "Someone is in here."

"Cool, let's ask him how to get out of this overheated sauna."

I couldn't agree more.

"What are you doing in the demon swamps?" An earth elemental materialized, covered in mulch.

He had chocolate eyes and a medium-brown complexion that matched the muddy dirt. In place of hair, green vines sprouted from his head. He had hooves much like tree roots instead of feet.

"We're lost." Brigit placed her hands on her hips and bit her bottom lip. Then we both heard him and turned toward another tunnel.

"Firepower." The tree man took Brigit's hand and brought it to his mouth.

A glassy stare came over her as he brushed his fingers across her cheeks and down her slender throat.

"Brigit, Celtic fire nymph. You are a beauty. A fire gem, which I rarely see in this area."

My heart pounded, sensing that someone had trapped us. "Your name?" I snapped, not at all liking the desire I saw in his eyes as he gazed at Brigit.

"My name is Yarrow Swampland."

"There's no originality in that last name." I couldn't hold back my sarcasm.

"Well, Yarrow, we'd appreciate some help. Could you lead us to the doorway back into the human realm?" Brigit gave him her hottest smile.

"You've trespassed into the underworld, and once here, rarely does one leave. Today, you're in luck." He held Brigit's hand a moment longer than he should.

I faced a murky stairway that wasn't there a moment ago. A misty umber haze appeared in front of the mud-caked wall. "Uplic. Ocriot. Praekanian."

A whistling sound came from the portal, and the three of us stepped through into a bustling city. Restaurants lined the right side of the street, while clothing shops and various small businesses lined the other. Not what I expected of the underworld. The environment seemed too natural, too normal. An uneasy feeling aroused suspicion. My alarm bells rang loud and clear.

I gave an anxious little cough to get Brigit's attention. Brigit smiled and motioned for me to stop lagging.

I pointed to my head and mouthed, telepathy. Nothing.

"Where are we going?" Brigit's voice carried a velvet-edge. Her tone was vehement, with no fear or suspicion that something was definitely not right.

"My beautiful nymph, your friend has an appointment."

"What?" I blurted and stumbled back, dumbfounded.

"We're here."

Above me swung a sign. The Afterlife Brew was in a vast cavern, and phosphorescent fungi and glowing ghostly lights illuminated it. A rich aroma of dark-roasted coffee beans, mingling with an undercurrent of incense that drifted from smoky cauldrons bubbling with exotic elixirs.

A man in the far corner sat alone. His features were perfect, so symmetrical that any more delicacy would have made him too beautiful.

Yarrow turned to me.

His smile was without malice, almost apologetic.

I wiped my hands down my jeans, forgetting I wasn't wearing an apron. I'm sure a dazed expression crossed my face at the hilarity that someone in the underworld expected my arrival.

"He awaits you."

"With him?" I pointed my finger, not understanding. I caught his scent, and his smell reminded me of Uriel, but with a touch of sandalwood. Even the surrounding glow disappeared in contrast to the underground caverns. I imagined him flying in the clouds like an angel.

"Ms. Naesatra."

His greeting was a husky whisper that made him even more dangerous. Sexuality oozed from this man. I was sure women fawned all over him. His powerful allure pulled at my very alive libido. In an instant, he was in my mind and my body. Even using all my psychic powers against his invasion, I couldn't break his grip. I turned toward Brigit.

She glanced over her shoulder. "See you soon."

Panic rioted through me, watching my friend leave me alone. My thoughts fragmented as the fear and anger knotted inside me. "Where's Brigit going?"

"She left with Yarrow to visit our fine town."

"Who the muffin cakes are you?" I pulled a confinement potion from my fanny pack, ready to run. Hopefully, the potion would give me time to escape and find Brigit.

His lips quirked into a half-smile. "Leave the potion in your boot. I mean you no harm. In fact, I'm here to help you."

"Help me?" I sputtered. Was I losing my sensibility? Find the necromancy book if you're so eager to help." My attitude needed a makeover, but I didn't appreciate being deserted by my best friend. I bit my lower lip and stared, waiting for him to talk.

"Samael is my name."

"Do I know you?"

"I'm from Kumuria and live in the demon realm."

"You're an angel like Uriel." The last few days were the worst in my life. If I hadn't asked him to go to Wildelea, he wouldn't have disappeared.

"I am the seducer of both light and dark, whereas Luc and Uriel are the luminaries of humanity."

Seducer fit this pretty man. An oddly primitive warning sounded in my brain. Memories I couldn't quite grasp flashed into my mind. I blew my psychic shields in shreds while his thoughts, his power, swam inside my head. I put my hands to my ears. The ringing hurt, and I wanted it to end. "Stop!"

"Push into your gifts and open your mind and body. Embrace your Seidr power."

Lights vibrated all around me, and my body shimmered. The feeling pushed deep into my core, and the heat, desire, and horror all melded into one. I screamed.

"Call to your mate. Bring him here to work beside you."

Lights flowed in and out like an exploding star. Nausea threatened to consume me. "What's happening?"

"I've given you the strength of deflection and deviation with the ability to stop the active powers of others and return attacks to where they came from. Deflection magic will help you in your fight against Carman."

"Will you explain what is going on before I lose my peanuts and go postal?"

"A challenge occurred between Diablo and Yahweh."

"I already know about the wager. I want to know why my mother, Baal, and Dother want to take power? What are they after?" Wariness edged into the back of my thoughts. Why was he helping me instead of Uriel or Odin?

"The conflict between light and dark elves is an age-old dispute over rulership, much like Diablo and Yahweh's. Throughout the universe, the spirit shadow rises in every pantheon, prepared for the third coming. Only the kundalini can subdue the shadows lurking to overtake the light."

I wove my fingers through my knotted hair to make logical sense of all the tidbits of information.

"The kundalini curse is what Uriel called it. The torture of the five Sarim princes. When he'd relayed the story, I hadn't really taken him seriously. It sounded too far-fetched for angels." Now I felt the heart-pull, the calling of my other half, and I needed to see for myself that Uriel lived.

Samael chuckled with a dry, cynical laugh as he leaned back in his chair. "Drink your tea."

A cup appeared before me, steaming with a hint of cinnamon chai. My favorite. What else had he gathered about me on his journey inside my mind, body, and soul?

"Locate the third book, the one with the red jasper."

"My friend has hidden the book deep in the forest."

"Let the gem call to you. The other books are not the issue. Carman, Hagmer, Diablo, and Baal want you. The power to unlock the spell lives within you. The blood of the earth is in you. Your mother knew that when Hel, goddess of the cold, allowed your father to leave Niflheim with you. Carman gained access to her freedom through you, Moira. You've become her chance at resurrection." Too startled to utter a word, I remained in stunned silence.

My mouth grew dry. Samael's confirmation that Carman intended to sabotage my life and steal my magic screamed betrayal of the worst kind.

A shadow crossed over our table, and a chill sucked the oxygen from the room. My breath lodged behind the lump, closing my air passages.

His hand touched the top of my crown. "Drop your head between your legs and breathe." Samael ran his slender fingers through my curls and massaged the throbbing muscles at the nape of my neck. Closing my eyes, I melted into the magic oozing from his fingers. A calming sensation eased the tension, allowing me to gather my wits.

Images cleared. "Gramercy," I yelped in surprise at the strong feeling of relief coursing through me.

He chuckled. "Haven't heard the term used in centuries, mother goddess and Uriel's mate. I accept your thanks."

The calm feeling disappeared, and another surge of fear ripped through me.

"Push through your anxiety and accept that you are part of both the shadow and the light."

"Why are you hurting me with your words?" Distrust of the unknown dropped its anchor. I'd had too many unexpected surprises in the last few days and wanted to jump off the plank.

Even Brigit had slipped away with swamp man, leaving me alone to fend for myself. I'd give her a tongue thrashing as soon as she returned. I was tired and ready to go home.

"Diablo sent me here to prevent your reunion with Uriel. Diablo encourages the other gods to join in his quest against the light. Hundreds in all the pantheons prepare for the battle between the light and dark elves. Many will aid Carman in her pursuit of power. Diablo and Hagmer have signed blood agreements."

"Every time someone opens their mouth, the day gets worse." I pulled at my hair, confused and rather pissed off.

"Diablo wants to overpower his brother, but Yahweh holds the winning hand."

Samael studied me for a moment.

His grin was not the least bit apologetic as he laughed warmly and richly. "I like you."

"You like me?"

His smile faded. "Uriel ushers in the sunset and the ending day. He is the mirror of dreams, the source of strength, and the path to enlightenment."

I took a sip of my coffee to hide my reaction to his compliment. "Uriel's a tall glass of water to live up to. I'd never tell him, but I admire his tenacity."

"What is your relationship?"

I tossed him an uncertain look, at the gentleness of his gaze.

"I owe Uriel a favor." He let the words hang in the air without further explanation. "Beware; after today, I might not help you. Will you take the gift I offer right now for payment of my obligations to Uriel?" he whispered so faintly that I barely caught the words.

Thoughts raced in jumbled confusion as I struggled to figure out what he expected. Uriel mentioned Aurora, and the female part of him ripped from his spirit to live amongst the material realm of Earth.

"Why are you offering me help?"

"I admire Uriel."

"Then, why go against him?"

"I exist between the light and dark, belonging to neither."

"I don't understand."

He pulled out a pocket watch. "The witching hour. Will you make a bargain and accept the gift I offer?"

"What is my payment?" My nerves made my hands unsteady, so I flexed my fingers to dissipate the energy.

"One specialized cake."

I felt as if my emotions dangled over a vast chasm of confusion. His suggestion startled me too much to offer any objection. I gave a short laugh, filled with embarrassment that he'd bargain for one of my treats. "One cake, it is."

Unexpectedly, a blast of supernatural energy created a power shield around me. Colorful lights of brilliant, energetic magic danced like fireflies. I pulled a forest-green light from the swirling vortex and listened.

"Moira."

The nymph's voice was a symphony of music.

"Daughter of fate."

Before me stood a wood nymph dressed in hunter green leggings and a peach tunic, with her hair pulled into a stiff ponytail, which stood on the top of her head.

She offered a branch from Yggdrasil, the world tree of the Nordic realm. "You are the roots, the base, the earth," a chorus of voices sang in unison.

They vanished, and the words of Shakespeare's Macbeth seared into my mind. "By the pricking of my thumbs, something wicked this way comes." At the last words, a barrage of dark emotions tormented me. Images of my father tortured—the cruelty of their coupling, his anguished pain as Carman stole his sanity. Knowledge of his weakness frightened me as I watched my father, the warrior, beaten and stripped of his pride. I wanted to be somewhere else, not confronted with my own evil parent. I couldn't bear watching her steal his seed night after night until four children grew from her belly.

Samael stood. "Deflect my powers."

He mentally hauled me out of the chair. His green eyes turned to granite.

Pain crackled through my head, and I couldn't think with his energy signature pouring inside my mind. Purple, silver, and yellow flooded my essence. "No."

"Take control of your emotions. Weave your pain into a pattern that shields you."

Another blast of energy socked me in the stomach. Tears burned my eyes as I wanted to give up. I couldn't fight him. "Stop."

"Weave the magical energy and stop the assault. Deflect with the gift I gave you."

"I can't." The power hurt me, and I couldn't break free from the negativity pulling at my heart. My hands clenched under my left breast, wishing the sharp jolts would go away.

"Do it. Deflect the magic."

Daring me to defy him, he invaded my personal space and pushed me harder than I'd ever experienced. I froze in limbo, where all decisions and actions were impossible. My mind fragmented into a thousand different colors of excruciating pain. "You're killing me."

"If you don't block me, you will die. Now tap into the Nordic

Norns of your bloodline and call on their power. Use the deviation of the spell to undo the weave of magic."

"I'm trying." My abilities weren't strong enough to stop a Celtic witch as powerful as Carman.

"Stop me, or this breath will be your last because Carman will take your powers."

I gripped the branch and forced my spirit to journey through the nine worlds of Asgard to reach Yggdrasil. "I call on Urd, Verdandi, and Skuld, the Norns of fate. My fate is now in the hands of destiny. Urdr, that which is the past, Verdandi that which is the present—and Skuld that which is the future. I accept who I am and honor the gifts, and I call on the power of Seidr."

The intensity of energy surged, and pain tore at the fibers of my mind.

Samael sucked the life force right out of my body, ready to send me to Diablo.

I would die if I didn't fight back. But it hurt so much.

Inside my mind, Uriel's words penetrated through the fog. "Moira, believe in your light, believe you are my spirit-mate, and believe in your goodness. Become your destiny."

Uriel, with his obsidian wings and deep robin-egg eyes, held out his hands. His body blazed yellow and red. I reached for the light. If I could only grasp his fingers, I'd make it. Reaching deep into the very spirit of my soul, I emptied my mind and filled my body with a glorious white healing light. I resisted the pain.

Visualizing my magic's knot, I wove it into a blocking spell, fighting the emotions. To live, find Uriel, find that stone, and bring in the light were my goals. With one last blast from my mind, I slammed Samael out of my body, knocking him clear across the room. I took a quick breath of utter astonishment at seeing this powerful angel slammed against the wall.

His smile was alive with affection and delight.

Samael righted himself and walked over to me. "Your light magic shines. Uriel is a lucky man."

"I'm tired."

"Drink this. The shake is an elixir of root weed and lavender to restore balance."

I drank. "Am I protected against the dark?" I sat in the otherworldly cafe. Time felt fluid, and the burdens of the mortal realm faded, allowing the essence of life to be savored with each exquisite sip. I felt stronger and more capable. The trepidation of facing Carman lost its hold on me.

"That is a question only you can answer, but you fought me and won. You'll make Freya a strong Seidr priestess."

I reached over and touched his cheek. "Gramercy, my guardian angel."

"I have fulfilled my debt to Uriel." He pushed me toward the door. "Go to him. Study your magic, for if you are unprepared, you will not survive a battle against Carman."

Brigit and Yarrow came through the door.

Her flushed face spoke of excitement. "Moira, the city's beautiful. I never expected the underworld to thrive with so many shops and games of competition except in the torture arenas. The various legions compete for status and privileges."

I turned toward the table, then to Samael.

"The underworld has many layers, and not every fallen angel or demon intends harm. Within our own realm there are levels of light and dark, but beware, this place can be very dangerous when entered without permission and protection." Samael bade us goodbye and left the cafe.

Brigit stood beside Yarrow. "Ladies, it's been a pleasure, but you must return home," Yarrow said.

I followed him out of the coffeehouse and stepped through the portal back into the swamp, grasping Brigit's hand. "The doorway to your realm is through there."

"We can't leave. The book of dark arts." I frowned, looking down the river.

"Baal has the book, and he helps the necromancer. Break the summoning circle and deflect the necromancer's power over Valefor. Help will come."

"Thank you for the tour of the demon realm. Nicer than I expected," Brigit said.

"Fire goddess, you brightened a swamp man's heart."

"Let's go rescue Valefor and get the book of necromancy before they kill him."

Yarrow disappeared as Brigit and I stepped through the portal into Lycre's backyard.

Chapter Ten

URIEL

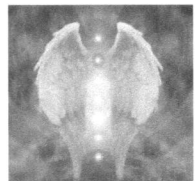

I parked my motorcycle on the side of the driveway. The roar of the barking huskies was loud enough to be heard a mile down the road. I stood at my bike, feeling guilty for leaving Moira alone for the last seven human days. But after I escaped the magical realm with the help of Gander's portal stone, I went to see my brothers to discuss the kundalini. I needed a few days to gather my wits and break down the wall of resentment that shadowed my thoughts.

First, we lost our archeia; now we're to reunite with our spirit-mates by making the females fall in love. I had no desire to be another pawn in Yahweh's games, but my brothers and I had little choice. If any of the five failed in locating the kundalini gem, we all faced losing our spirit-mates for all eternity. The Shekina of Yahweh would die, forever dooming mankind to live in separation from their female souls.

Going through the side gate, I heard voices from the other side of the gazebo. Moira, in black leggings and a purple tank, stole my breath. When Moira's gaze locked onto mine, relief washed over me. A thousand unspoken words sparkled as her glamour faded and her golden, ethereal aura glowed with happiness.

She charged forward and jumped into my arms. "Don't you ever scare me like that again. I thought you were dead."

Her beautiful amber eyes flamed with worry as her arms tightened around my neck and she kissed me. I whispered into her neck, "I missed you, too."

I waved to Lycre and Brigit.

Brigit tugged on Lycre's arm, pulling him inside the kitchen.

Moira and I stood alone underneath the canopy of trees. Her cheeks flushed pink. I wanted to devour her mouth and never let her go until she recognized me. I knew she understood, but until she accepted the claim with her heart and soul, we were still two people who could easily go our separate ways.

"Where were you?"

"There is a time difference that exists between the celestial and human realms."

"That's all you've got to say? A time difference?" An eyebrow lifted.

Our gazes battled for a long moment as she pressed her mouth into a tight line.

"You threw me into a burning fire and left me to figure it out on my own."

"Sorry. Making a fire ring was all I could think of to break the spell."

"How did you counteract the magical weave they used to trap us within Wildelea?"

"The flaming sword used the element of fire to find the weakness within the spell."

"You left me." I blew out my breath and ruffled a stray red curl from her forehead.

"I went to Kumuria with every intention of immediately returning to Ventura. But my brothers gave me rather disturbing news."

"More about the curse?"

My brow shot up, realizing she wouldn't understand. None of our archeia would recognize the males as their kindred mates. Each man must make a female fall in love with him. I expected failure, my heart cold and unlovable. "Indirectly."

"I met a friend of yours, and he said that he's paid his debt."

"Samael." Her eyes brightened, and my heart sagged with a feeling of despair, seeing the pleasure written in the smile she gave.

"What did he want?" I narrowed my eyes, curious how Moira had met Samael.

"The story's rather long. Come join everyone in the backyard."

I followed as she ran her fingers through the red plants she had adored during our initial visit. I tried to remember what she called them. Hummingbird sage.

Lycre came out the patio door carrying a platter full of ribs. Brigit followed. "Wondered if I needed to send out a search party."

"Uriel, get a beer and keep these ribs from burning while I finish slicing the tri-tip."

Moira, with no embarrassment, planted a kiss on me.

"Help with dinner. I need to check on Brigit and Munin's progress with the summoning circle."

I grabbed her arm before she could leave. "You're not intending to call in any demon legions, are you?"

"We're going after Bael, but at the moment we're not strong enough; we need Katrina's magic."

"Are you out of your mind?"

"She's not." Lycre said, "I'm going to Alfheim to speak with Freyr and find out how Carman uses the mares before we risk any lives. Katrina will return with me, and then they're going to follow Valefor into the underworld."

Thunderstruck, I released her arm as she moved toward the other women. Lycre rang the dinner bell. Piles of food filled the patio table, and everyone greedily ate as if it were their last supper.

Uriel picked up their plates. "You're not going back to the underworld."

"We're planning on going within the next day." Moira wrapped her arms around her best friend. "Brigit, be careful at the house. Trolls are lurking, so don't make yourself a target."

Brigit's palms lit with the fire dragon's blood. No doubt she could handle a few trolls without skipping a beat.

"I could use a good fight. I hoped one of those pesky irritants would stroll onto the property. It'll give me practice." Brigit turned and winked at me. "How's that handsome brother of yours?"

"Luc fine. He told me to relay the message You've got some explaining to do."

Brigit smirked. "How'd he like his little surprise?"

"A fire-dragon ring on the left nipple. Nice. You know, his branding might just leave you sizzling at what he'll do to you."

"The ring and its power are a fair trade for the key." She tapped the pendant around her neck. "If he can handle the heat, we'll see if he can play."

My brother might have met his match. "You're full of witty tricks from the kiss left on my brother's groin."

"A promise for another day."

I set the plates on the counter. If she and Luc were kindred spirits, Yahweh had a crude sense of humor. In finding Moira, I recognized her essence and wanted to consummate our relationship. My body craved hers, but I'd lived with this loneliness for too many years. I wasn't the man I used to be, instead more of a shadow.

I bade the others good day, and the three of us exited the rear yard and moved into the garages. Brigit climbed into the red Jaguar. "I'm going to Kildare to talk with Ecne, my cousin, regarding your situation."

"Send him my regards and tell him I owe him a scotch." I wrapped my arm around Moira's shoulders.

Moira handed her the keys and kissed her on the cheek. "Inside the pantry in the yellow tin are your father's favorite pecan wafers. Take them."

"OMG, you spoil everyone. What about Ecne? He'll have a fit if I don't bring him those butterscotch candy drops."

I had to chuckle that Ecne, a man I respected and admired, fell to the mercy of Feathery Bakery's charm. Was any celestial or magical not in love with these baked treats?

"Check in the fridge. Tell him I'll create a special batch of bread with funnel grains, just the way he likes them."

"See you around," Brigit called out the window as she backed out of the driveway.

"You wouldn't have any white cake?" Her cakes tasted like the softest, creamiest vanilla.

"No, but I'll make a special recipe for you." She slid behind me on my motorcycle and spoke into the headset. "I'll even add my secret potion with cream cheese icing." Her words purred in my ear.

I lifted the kickstand, and the engine roared to life. I sucked in a deep breath. Maybe I'd wait on pushing her for more information training until after dessert. Her cakes tasted of sunshine, hope, and love.

Chapter Eleven

MOIRA

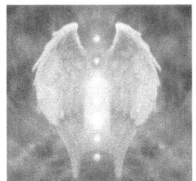

Lust for Uriel burned in my brain, and I could think of nothing else. A powerful magnetic voltage, an intensity stronger than both of us, pulled me to him. A force I had to fight before I lost myself in those green eyes dancing with flame. I yearned to feel and take like I'd never experienced with another man. Yet, his intensity scared me, his presence over-whelmed me, and his emotional distance worried me. "Uriel, let's go inside." A car went past, reminding me we leaned against his motorcycle.

He grasped the back of my neck and brought his mouth to mine. "I want you in my arms tonight." I followed him up the staircase. I had to bake. Baking allowed me to explore my feelings, and I needed to process the desires consuming me. I took my overnight bag and retrieved my favorite baking dress. "Where's your bathroom?"

"Through the kitchen is a washroom."

Uriel set the bags on the table. "I've got a phone call to make."

"Okay." I changed clothes. Feeling refreshed, I unpacked the food and put the dinner supplies in the fridge. I lined up my herbs in order of their use, then I pulled out my bottle of pure vanilla bean extract and potions to make the white cake Uriel wanted.

My life felt so different after coming back from Wildelea, something within me changed, a part of me unlocked, and I did not understand how to manage the newfound strength inside me. Sexual spell combinations popped into my thoughts and my libido raged. I couldn't fight the raw attraction to the man before me or fight the need to help my father and now, with the sacred blue moon ceremony in two weeks, I had to find the grimoire. I had to learn the secrets hidden within the pages of Seidr's sacred text and learn the words of the ceremonial blessing.

I'd left the academy in search of Valefor, thinking I'd have the book within a day. Instead, I caused my dearest friend to lose her shop. Dother took the second book to commit his heinous crimes and I was still no closer to finding the third book of magic.

Uriel came into the kitchen and stopped. "What's wrong?"

"Not a thing." I bit my lip to stifle the outcry of desperation, fighting to choke the life right out of me. The sour twist of his mouth showed that he didn't believe me. I blocked my mental shields. This close, Uriel could easily read the lie.

Tears formed in the back of my eyes. I baked when my deepest emotions came to the surface. Based on my volcanic eruption, my father and Uriel were equally on my mind. "Just overwhelmed. It's nothing."

He took me into his arms and cradled me against his chest, allowing me to release the feelings inside. I placed my hand on his chest and soaked in the warmth of his body. "Thank you."

"Anytime. I need to finish some paperwork. Will you be all right for half an hour?"

"I'll be fine now that I've let it out." I shooed him away and took a minute to take in his home.

The contemporary style didn't fit my expectations. I imagined an earthier environment instead of the clean, modern architecture found in the newer designs. A large window adorned the side wall that overlooked historical downtown Pasadena. The kitchen was at the rear of the room with a sliding door that opened to an outdoor patio. In the front room, a large gaming center filled the entire wall. When I noticed a half-read James Patterson book upside down on the arm of the chair, I smiled.

Snooping in his kitchen cabinets, I found a sauté skillet and bundt pan. For two bachelors, they kept a well-equipped kitchen, which surprised me.

I combined flour and a special blend of sugar with a touch of vanilla. In the palm of my hands, I mixed the following to create a special potion for our night together. A pinch of angelica for magic, mugwort for tranquility, pansy for happy thoughts, and sunflower for protection. My own sensitivities poured into the mixture with each swipe of the spoon, giving the cake a sparkle of love.

I could heal with my cakes, as the effects of my potions responded to the individual's desire. Throughout the realms and other pantheons, my cakes made thousands happy. Too bad I couldn't prevent the dark elves from desiring Freyr's kingdom as easily as I could cheer up a despondent mood. I pushed down the bristling sentiment and tapped into elated feelings of happiness. Images of a calm lake and green meadows filled with sweet-smelling lavender replaced the dark melancholy that threatened me earlier. Being an earth elf, I fed off emotions. Emotions carried our hopes, and in Uriel's cake, I planned to infuse laughter. In the crumb cakes, I'd included a dash of optimistic hope in our search for Valefor.

I placed the cake pans in the oven, set the timer for thirty minutes. In a separate bowl, I combined the batter for the crumb cake I'd take to Ventura. Next, I opened the cream cheese and whipped up a delectable frosting for Uriel's cake. I covered the bowl and put the icing in the fridge until after dinner.

Done for the moment, I stepped outside on the patio and took in the city. Old town Pasadena was beautiful with its quaint streets. A comforting breeze tickled my arms like a butterfly whisper. I loved this area, but suddenly, my scalp pricked, I stopped to listen for magical or human intruders. In my heightened state, danger seemed right around the corner. I almost jumped over the railing when Uriel's voice bellowed in the kitchen.

"Is this my cake?"

I turned toward him in time to see him dip his finger into the mixture, and I rushed through the sliding glass doors.

"It's crumb cake for breakfast." I looked back over the city, and the nervous sensation disappeared, making me question my sanity. "Pour us a glass of wine and I'll start cooking the salmon. The white cake's baking for another ten-minutes."

"I can't wait."

His strong, velvet-edged voice made me want to attack him right there on the kitchen floor.

He brought me a glass of Chardonnay. His mouth brushed against my lips. "Don't hide from me, elfin princess. Not tonight!" He wandered into the living room, leaving me to stand in the kitchen panting with desire and uncertainty.

What if Uriel only wanted my body and couldn't love the real me? I knew we were mates, but the idea that this angel could destroy my emotional foundation, leaving me broken-hearted, caused me to withdraw inside my protective safe place and throw away the key.

His confidence regarding our destiny intimidated me. I didn't believe in that kind of enduring love. In Alfheim, the longevity of life interfered. A couple staying together for an eternity without taking lovers was a rare gift.

Tonight, I'd find out. A warm glow flowed through me, thinking of what his hot mouth and powerful hands would do to my body.

Uriel turned on the gaming console, and NBA Playground 2 appeared on the wall screen.

"No fair! Foul ball." I thrust my fist in the air and stood behind him.

He tilted his head up and laughed.

"Here!" He handed me a gaming handle.

I shot a free throw, making the basket. "Hot tamale, I'm good," I shouted and handed it back.

The timer rang, and I returned to the kitchen and took the cake out of the oven, setting it on the counter to cool. An aroma of vanilla filled the kitchen and tantalized the senses. I closed my eyes, imagining the cake melting in my mouth like the sweetest of cream.

"Smells good."

Following him out the sliding door, I hoped the feeling of being watched disappeared. I set the platter of cheese and crackers on the table and took in the view. The drifting clouds picked up deeper pinks and purples with a touch of orange as the sun slid toward the San Gabriel Mountains.

"What made you move to Sierra Madre?"

"When I started my bakery in the human realm, I wanted a place that radiated life, the spirit of the forest, and the oneness of the community." I inhaled a deep refreshing breath. "You've got a wonderful view of the mountains."

"I was thrilled when we found the loft. The patio's positioned at a perfect angle to catch the evening view." He flapped his hands at the beautiful scenery.

"I'm curious. Why do you live in the human realm?"

His body tightened at the question. "After the great celestial war, when the heavens and earth separated, many angels left Kumuria and joined Diablo in the underworld. Some migrated to other pantheons. We created the demon realm after the fall. Most occupants comprise the fallen angels who sided with humanity against Yahweh. They became testers of faith."

"And the angels that stayed in Kumuria?"

"We became guardians and watchers."

"You're a guardian?" Somehow, the protector fit this powerful angel, who didn't see the pure beauty of his soul. I felt his grief over losing Jacobson's case, making me want to ease his pain and melt the ice surrounding his heart.

"Yes, each of us has special skills. Luc and I practice law. We stamp out injustice where we can. My brother, Mikael's a warrior, Ananiel's a watcher of the Nephilim children. In your lands, he's known as a giant."

I sat back in my seat, watching the daylight close its eyes and push the world into evening. My thoughts drifted, wishing we could stay in this perfect cocoon for a little longer. "I haven't frosted the cake. Would you like to help?"

Uriel's face lit up like Christmas. "Can I ask you a question?"

"Sure."

"How many brothers do you have?" I took the frosting from the fridge and set it on the counter to warm to room temperature.

"My father had twelve sons. Five of us are Sarim princes."

"And the other seven? Well, Luc represents all energies, and the others are leaders of the Archangel domains, much like the leaders of the mortal world. My curiosity piqued. I wanted to understand more about his life and the angelic realm.

His world did not differ from my own, as images of Carman and my brothers filled my thoughts. Fate played cruel jokes. If Uriel and I were kindred spirits, I'd been a pawn on the chessboard for a long time. The injustice filled my heart, and part of me wanted revenge on those who thought they had a right to play with our lives.

"Where are your thoughts?" The muscles in his jaw clenched. He appeared ready to defeat any that threatened to harm me.

Sensing his distress and need, I touched his arm. "Thinking about what will happen when I face Carman." I dipped my finger into the buttercream frosting I'd infused with hope. "Can I stop Carman before she escapes Niflheim?"

"What do you know of your powers?"

I'd been waiting for him to broach the subject since my visit with Samael. "In the last twenty-four hours, images and psychic premonitions appeared in my waking mind. The other day, I spoke with the squirrels and understood their language. My weaves of magic are unbreakable, and the potions hold more strength. I hear voices of those who've crossed over to the underworld asking for a new destiny and a rebirth. I hold the power to offer them their desire-part of the Seidr gifts given through the three Norns of Odin."

"Also, the gift of the necromancers to bring back or communicate with the dead."

He dropped a dollop of icing onto the cake and spread the cream along the sides. "Any confrontation with black magic?"

His lip curled into a look of faint amusement, like he already had his answer.

"Just the darkness. Samael pushed at me." My mind struggled to assimilate the new powers that allowed me to enter the realm of the Seidr priestesses and shaman healers of the spirit world. Was I strong enough to tap into the tapestry of these special sacred women capable of changing the weave of destiny and life?

"They embed your magic roots with the ancient Vikings. Your psychic lines with the Norns of destiny connect you to the world tree of life."

"If Carman escapes her imprisonment in Niflheim, we all lose." I patted my lap, unsure of how I felt about all I'd learned.

"You alone have the power to unlock the spell of the three books. You, my love, must learn to use all your abilities. Tonight is the first step to learning your true birthright."

Uriel's expression held a touch of sadness. "The situation scares me." A shudder of apprehension rippled down my back at the intimacy.

"Our bonding will allow you access to my powers. Together, we can fight and bind her to Odin's prison for all of eternity."

My skin tingled at the serious pleading in his tone. A laugh slipped out at the absurdity of my life crashing around me. "If we're kindred spirits, shouldn't I be head-over-heels in love with you?"

"You're not?" He grabbed a handful of chocolate almonds from a nearby bowl. "Well, I wager that tomorrow morning you'll be begging me to marry you during the new moon festival."

"Cocky, aren't you?" What if he was right? If I gave in to these feelings, I'd have to risk my heart and trust he wouldn't abandon me.

His chuckle was low, throaty, and I admired his belief in me, the willingness to risk it all for a woman he barely knew. Yet, if the flame in his eyes meant anything, I was already his woman. The rest was a formality. "This arrangement you've created in your head has a few flaws."

He reached over and rubbed my cheek. "Trust me."

"What if my darker side takes over?" Uriel breached the barriers of my mind, sending up his own interpretation.

Listen.

I leaned back and fought the warning voice whispering in my head. I didn't want to know the global picture and the images of the kundalini, the ancient curse, and my father's bondage. Images of the Norns at their spindles, threads of woven patterns of destiny, and a darkness taking power over the realms. Thousands of years of bondage if we failed in our journey, and Diablo and the dark elves gaining control of the kundalini gems.

"Let your mind sleep and spend the night with me."

My heart triple-beat as I visualized this beautiful man in my bed, and heat flushed my face.

Uriel continued to frost the cake, giving me a few minutes to gather my thoughts. A strange awareness of finding my one true love struck me as ironic. Uriel wouldn't be my first lover. Yet, I was like a young innocent awaiting their first time. My blood throbbed in my veins with desire when he took my hand.

"I want a piece of cake."

I sliced a section and placed it on a plate. Using a fork, I offered him a bite. His gaze never left mine as he chewed the cake and smiled. His eyes flamed as he took the plate from my hand, set it on the table, and pulled me into his arms.

My mind reeled with anticipation and confusion. Tension burned between my legs. I wanted him. Taking a needed breath, I assembled my raging hormones into some kind of order. I had a feeling once I surrendered to this man, my life would belong to him. I just didn't know if I was ready to make that choice.

Chapter Twelve

URIEL

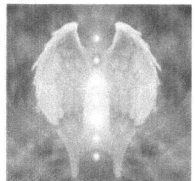

I ate the last bite of cake and set the fork down, my fingers trembling. Moira's face was beautiful with those high cheekbones, the gentle curve of her lips, and I couldn't tear my eyes from hers. Dessert dishes waited in the sink, but all I felt was a hollow rumble between my legs, a summons I hadn't obeyed in centuries.

She drifted behind me, warm fingertips tracing circles across my shoulders. The press of her hand sent a spark down my spine, and instinct overrode reason. I spun, pinning her against the cool tile of the kitchen wall. Her breath hitched. A flicker of amber light danced in her pupils, betraying the fire she tried to hide.

Heat beaded along my skin. I wanted her soul, her body, every secret tucked beneath that sunflower-yellow dress. My hand slid down her back, the fabric shifting until I felt the smooth warmth of her skin. Moira's dress pooled at her ankles, and she stepped free of it, the fabric whispering against tile. She wore nothing underneath, no barrier between us but the thrill that charged the air.

I pressed my mouth to the column of her throat, tasting salt and honey. Her arms wrapped around my neck, drawing me closer. When my palm landed on her inner thigh, she shivered, hips tilting into my palm, offering herself. A tremor ran through her. "Uriel," she breathed, voice fragile as spun silk.

I traced my thumb along the swell of her breast, then cupped the hardness I found there. Her back arched; she drew a ragged breath and tilted her chin up to meet my lips. Every nerve ending ignited as we grazed and slipped together, a dance older than time. I slipped two fingers between her folds, teasing, and she let out a small cry that echoed in my bones.

Our bodies moved in rhythm: kiss, touch, gasp. Lightning curled through my chest as I curled inside her, my fingers pressing into her center, coaxing moans that tasted of longing. When she caught my finger, waved it, rolled her hips, I knew she needed me as much as I needed her. I curled my fingers, chasing that tiny knot of pleasure, and her back arched so hard her heels lifted off the floor.

She clutched my shoulders, lost in the swirl of sensation. I leaned forward, mouth ghosting over her ear. "Mine," I whispered, and the word slipped between us like a promise.

Her heat grounded me, even as blood pounded through my veins. When Moira's knees gave way, I lifted her, gathering her in my arms as if she weighed nothing at all, and carried her down the hall to my bedroom. The door clicked shut behind us, and the moon glow pooled at our feet, painting her skin silver.

I set her on the mattress and let desire war with reverence. My shirt joined her discarded dress in a crumpled heap; I flicked on a lamp, soft light spilling over rumpled sheets. I reached for the condom in my drawer, my hands unsteady now that the moment had arrived. I kneeled between her thighs, paused, her eyes met mine, flame still shining there.

"When I enter you, our spirits will bind," I whispered. "You'll feel me in every heartbeat. I have sealed my soul to yours."

She swallowed hard, fingers curling into the sheet. "I," Her gaze budged, indecision flashing behind her lashes. She drew in a breath, her chest rising and falling. "Uriel, I need to know if I choose this," she said, voice steady.

My chest clenched. I had assumed the bond was fate, was fire. But here she was, offering me the gift of her consent. I nodded once, hard. "I will wait for your choice, for your heart."

Relief bloomed across her face, softening the lines of fear and anger I'd seen earlier. She reached for my hand and pressed it to her chest, over a heart that pounded like a drum. I kissed her palm, then her fingertips, learning the texture of her skin.

She rolled onto her side so that her back curled against me. I slid my arm around her waist, tucking her close. Outside, the night was silent, as if the world itself held its breath. I laid a gentle kiss on Moira's temple. Her lashes fluttered; exhaustion pulled at her limbs.

"Sleep," I murmured. "We'll face tomorrow together." Her head sank into the hollow of my shoulder, and I felt her heartbeat slow. In that steady thrum I recognized home, two souls finding their way back to each other. And as her breathing deepened, I whispered into her hair, "Goodnight, my Moira."

Chapter Thirteen

MOIRA

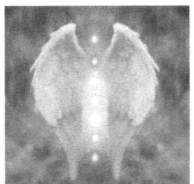

I clawed through the dark vines wrapping around my body. The net of tree limbs slithered over my legs, pulling me deeper into the dark, musky earth. The vines tightened around my torso, and I gasped for air, reaching for my last breath. I'd failed to stop the darkness from invading the light elfin realm. My mother was burying me alive. Overwhelming loss consumed my soul. I'd let down those I loved. I left the tattered, burned ruins of Alfheim behind. Ashes to ashes, dust to dust. "Noooo."

"Wake up."

Uriel's voice carried the cry of a strangled beast.

His hands clasped my shoulders, and he shook me with enough strength to wake the dead.

I reached toward his chest. "Stop shaking me!"

He brushed the wet smears from my cheeks.

I clung to his shoulders with my head resting on the pillow. I glanced around the room, realizing I was in Uriel's bed.

"Where were you?"

I couldn't allow him to witness my fear and nestled my face against his warm, firm chest. His arm wrapped around my shoulder, snuggling me closer.

"I had another bad dream." I snuffled. "My dreams were of the forbidden forest hidden deep within the islands of Japan. In the past year, we never saw again those who traveled to the sacred magical territories of the forbidden glen. Every pantheon fears the pre-historic markings of sacrifice and death in this ancient forest."

"How long have you been having these nightmares?"

"For a few weeks." Darkness folded over me, and I felt the same premonition of fear gasping softly in the dark as my thoughts centered on Uriel and hung on for dear life. I slowly lifted my head. "Carman's sending me dream messages. She uses the mare to haunt me and weaken my resolve through dream imagery."

His large hand cupped my face as his eyes narrowed. "None of your potions help?"

"Carman's magic unraveled every spell I'd used to block her from the dream landscape."

Uriel looked at the clock on the nightstand. "We've got three hours before we meet the others. Get showered." His fingers trailed along my cheeks, and he gently kissed my lips. "I'll keep you safe. You have my word.

I believed him. That's what scared me. I didn't want Uriel to sacrifice his life for mine. If Carman realized we were spirit-mates, she could use him against me. Every fiber in my body screamed for him to leave before Carman attacked him to destroy me.

I turned the shower to hot, planning to blast my skin into a cherry pink and let the coldness of my dreams wash down the drain. Taking a deep breath, I released the anxiety clouding my mind. I stepped from the shower. Wrapping the Turkish towel around my body, I relished the soft cotton that reminded me of a day at the spa. I took a speculative look around his bedroom. The deep burgundy hues stood out against the cream-colored walls. The environment reminded me of a dragon's den with treasured figurines of wild animals. Repurposed metal grates fronted his end table. A perfect room for his fiery nature. Warmth encompassed the space, so like the man. Running a finger along the leather bed frame, I could guess he paid top dollar. I picked up his dagger from the wall unit, swinging my arm as I accidentally tossed the feather-light knife behind me.

"Whoa, careful." Uriel jumped out of the knife's trajectory.

"Sorry, thought it'd be heavy."

"The blade's meant to kill swiftly."

I pulled the knife out of carpet and put the dagger back on the shelf, self-conscious of his gaze.

Uriel set a mug of coffee on the dresser.

"Thanks." I tightened the towel around me, feeling uncomfortable and somewhat vulnerable.

"I made scrambled eggs and ham." He stepped out of the room and closed the door.

His aquamarine eyes, filled with such pain, tore at my heart. We hadn't talked about last night, and I knew my rejection stung, but I couldn't risk our involvement. Love caused people to make choices they normally wouldn't consider. To have him think I didn't have feelings for him was better.

Satisfied with my self-talk, I slipped on a pair of black leggings, black flat boots, and a pink tank top. I was ready for battle in my standard go-to outfit. I had a feeling today would probably be the last peaceful one for a very long time.

From my backpack, I removed sage, bay laurel leaves, and rue oil, then tucked them into my pouch. I didn't want to be without the oil's enhancement properties. If I found myself trapped near the boundary of the underworld, I'd need the banishment oil close by in case any of the dead escaped.

Uriel knocked on the door. "Food's getting cold."

"I'll be right out." I put on my slave ring made from the finest metals and woven with dwarf magic. My ring served as a protector shield since it had the power to steal a person's gifts.

A new sensation surged through my body, and I felt more like a bad-ass warrior like Freya and Brigit, not the gentle baker and potion-maker. I'd always envied her easy way with the sword, her satiric nature, and her ballsy attitude when doing whatever she wanted. Freya carried the same free spirit and had no problem racing her chariot of cats through the center of town. To embrace that warrior side of my nature felt freeing.

I took a last look around the room and picked up my discarded clothes, placing them in my bag.

Uriel sat at the table, swiping his finger across his iPad. He glanced at me and looked back at the tablet.

I sat next to him and devoured my breakfast, not sure what to say. I rinsed my plate and put it in the dishwasher.

Uriel stood.

"Ready?"

"Do you have a plastic container for the crumb cake?"

He rummaged through the bottom cabinet and held out a Glad rectangular bowl.

I wrapped the cake and gathered my belongings.

He locked the door, and we punched the elevator for the ground floor. On the way out, he waved to the doorman.

A silence lingered between us. What was there to say?

Uriel placed the crumb cake in the saddlebag, along with my clothes. He handed me the helmet and looked at me with cold, tired eyes.

The traffic to Ventura was light this time of the morning. We'd left Pasadena after rush hour and reached the 101 Freeway in record time. The hour went by without incident. The calmness worried me. I darted my gaze in all directions, expecting visitors since we traveled along a parallel border between the shifters, elementals, and humans.

The clouds drifted lazily, creating animal or word formations. In childhood, I used to sneak into the Sierra Madre forest. I'd lie on my back, using the wildflowers as my bed, and watch the human children play in the stream that ran under the mythical crossover bridge. The elves formed villages where shoppers of both realms found unique treasures, and the local witches in the area came to meditate and commune with nature.

Uriel swerved to the right and exited at Ventura Boulevard.

I tensed.

We crossed into shifter lands, and Odin's ravens, Hugin and Munin, flew beside us, spreading their ebony wings and moving like graceful hang-gliders. As the crows merged with Uriel to the side of the road, two squawks came from Hugin, telling me Odin wished to speak with me.

Since my visit with Samael, I have gained the ability to understand languages. A talent I'm sure would help me.

The two ravens shifted into their human forms and trekked toward us.

Uriel removed his helmet and stepped away from the motorcycle. He followed Hugin as they walked along the gravel roadside.

The neighing of a horse overhead made me look into the sky.

Odin, with his long beard and conical helmet with protruding horns, rode his massive stallion, Sleipnir.

His gaze seared into me. As a little girl, I'd only seen Odin when he came to the autumn festivals or needed Freya's warriors. When he swooped down from the ridge of the otherworld's realm right for me, dread filled me. "Crispy donuts, he's gonna pluck me right from this road."

The last vision I saw was Uriel flying after us with murder in his eyes, trailed by two midnight-blue ravens.

Chapter Fourteen

URIEL

I stood there and watched as Odin, on his mighty winged horse, Sleipnir, swept Moira from the ground, placing her in front of him before taking to the skies. My own six wings sprouted, prepared to go after them.

"Odin's here to take her to Valhalla, the land of slain warriors. She needs to learn to fight." Munin tried her best to calm me down, but the fury in the one-eyed god caused me to tremble with dread.

"I will teach her. She should be with me."

Hugin cocked his head in the horizon's direction. "Odin's the ruler of the Nordic pantheon, and he decides. If he demands to train one of his people, it will happen."

I grunted, for I was in the Nordic shifter territory as Lycre's guest. If Odin banished me, I'd lose all contact with her. Challenging his authority was a terrible idea.

"I need Moira to complete the pentagram to save Valefor."

"Loki, the god of thievery, will lend his help in keeping Valefor alive. Baal and Dother drained the demon duke's blood. Go, seraphim, and help the others until Moira returns." Hugin pushed me back towards my bike.

I rubbed my pectoral muscle and felt a stabbing in the sensitive flesh. The scar had grown tender since she'd refused the mating call. I feared her death.

"Your spirit-mate has traveled the darkness alone."

Munin's sharp tone caused me to grimace. Her words paralyzed me. How had she known Moira denied the mating ritual that would have given her the powers of my light?

"I will not abandon her."

Moira screamed.

Without hesitation, I flew after them through the doorway into the land of the dead.

At the border, Odin's horse reared, and Moira fell into Valhalla.

I brandished my flaming sword, ready to gouge out his heart for his treacherous act. Odin turned and faced me.

"You may not enter Valhalla. She is a Seidr necromancer priestess and will survive the land of the dead. If you trespass, you will give up your life and open the gates of Ragnarok," he roared across the vast arena of clouds.

I fought the searing burn beneath my breast with agonizing torture. The scar threatened to split open my chest. My heart and soul wanted Moira.

"Your mate denies you. She refuses to embrace the future. Before she faces the Norn witches, she must rise and accept her destiny to help you recover the red jasper gem and take her place as goddess of all the pantheon."

If either of us lost our lives. Diablo would control the angels, the earthly humans, and the demon realms. Days of darkness unleashed would affect the other pantheons, creating a cosmic cataclysm.

"I need more time to convince her."

"At sunrise, Moira will face the warriors in Valhalla. She will fight until sundown. If she lives, meet her in Alfheim."

Odin's voice held the authority of a god used to his orders being followed.

"Odin, your warriors will kill her." My anger faded and a sick knot of tension coiled in my gut.

"She carries the Seidr magic to survive, but she lacks the confidence inside her. She trivializes her abilities and doesn't see that her witch's magic was always stronger than the others."

"She's alone." I flexed my fingers to release the tension building in me.

"Is she?" Odin's beefy hand gripped his long, thick white beard. "Continue your search. If Valefor dies, Carman will gain power over his legions."

I flapped my lower wings, keeping my body stable against the breeze threatening my balance. "What are you not saying?"

Odin raised his spear high in the sky. "Loki will meet you in Ventura. Go!" He faced Sleipnir toward the great Viking hall and disappeared.

I landed next to my bike where Munin and Hugin shifted into human form beside me.

"What happened last night?" Munin asked. "We expected the kundalini dragon to rise at dawn."

I avoided her gaze, never had I failed with a woman, and admitting defeat was difficult. Munin, like most women, pried and brought it up like it was my fault.

"She said no."

"Ahh, what did you do? Forget to ask her?" Munin lifted her delicate brow.

"The others are waiting in Lycre's kitchen. Brigit said not to forget the crumb cake. She claims Moira fills the sweet treats with enticing magic." Hugin licked his lips.

"Do Brigit and Katrina know you and Moira are kindred spirits?" Munin asked.

"Brigit suspects we are involved, but I doubt either realizes the true significance." I snatched my helmet from my bike, totally frustrated at my inability to help Moira.

"The mating ritual. Bet's on it won't be long before lots of banging occurs between you and the lovely Seidr."

"Doubt that. She's not interested in the long term." I clenched my fist, trying to fight back the desire to punch something.

The ravens gave each other a knowing glance. "The wager between your species will affect the rest of the nine Nordic worlds. Mate with the woman or the curse of the twelve will never end."

"I've tried." My entire body vibrated with tension.

"Bring Katrina and Brigit into your confidence. They'll help."

I groaned. The last thing I wanted was two interfering women involved in my sex life.

"I can handle my own affairs."

"On the night of the Moon Festival, Odin expects Carman to disrupt the ceremony of the priestess. Katrina and Brigit will be your conduit to reach Moira, should Carman overtake her mind," Hugin said.

"Katrina and Brigit wait for our arrival." Munin chuckled. "Those three are an interesting triquetra of women."

"Has Loki arrived at Lycre's house?"

Hugin turned to Munin, scratched his chin, weighing the question.

"He'll arrive within the hour. He is a disgusting chap, with his snide overture that we owe him homage. What does Odin see in him?" Munin complained.

"We need you and Luc to search the realms for Dother. In the meantime, Loki will break Valefor from the hold Baal uses to bind him to the circle." Hugin nodded and shifted into his raven form, taking off toward Lycre's.

Knowing the women would be safely away from the pentagram and Baal's control, I let out a breath, relief filling my mind. I headed toward my motorcycle, feeling helpless. I had to clear the fog from my thoughts. Once on the bike, I revved my engine and did a three-quarter wheelie, leaving a black streak along the highway. I tore past the trees and took the switchbacks farther into the hills. I wanted a moment to myself before facing a squad of people who'd blame me for Moira being kidnapped and thrown into Valhalla.

My prime aim was to keep her alive. If she lived, I'd make her see why we belonged together.

A small dog dodged onto the road, causing me to turn the bike toward the drop-off to my right and brake. Shit, I almost ran over the small blur of fur.

The pup quickly dashed to the side of the road and turned onto its back. The puppy couldn't be more than eight weeks old. A golden retriever, if my assumptions were correct.

I parked my bike and walked over to the little fellow. His tail wagged uncontrollably, and I picked him up. I didn't see any houses where he might have escaped. Alone on the road, the pup was vulnerable, and I couldn't leave him. Instead, I tucked him into my shirt and patted his bottom. As he curled around my waist, he squeaked sounds of pleasure.

Back on my bike, I continued to Lycre's house at a slower speed so I wouldn't scare the pup, sleeping against my stomach. My frustration vanished with the appearance of the dog. As an angel, I created distractions or small interventions that led a person on their fated path. Creating a doorway was my way to help Moira survive Odin's warriors, but I couldn't control her decisions.

I parked in the driveway, leaving my helmet in the saddlebag. I walked into the backyard. A cry came from Katrina. Brigit and Katrina dashed toward me. When a tiny bark came out, they stopped and lifted a brow. I released the pup from my jacket.

Lycre's huskies caught the scent of an outsider and rushed over to investigate. The dogs prodded the little one with their noses, deciding whether they'd accept him. A dog required far more care than a cat. Serena, the office cat, maintained herself and controlled us. An idea grew on me as the puppy wagged its tail in complete happiness. I'd give him to Moira. Maybe she could create a spell allowing him to cross over into both realms. He'd make a perfect protector.

"Where's Moira?" Brigit looked behind me.

"Odin's taken her to Valhalla to fight the warriors until sunset."

"You let him take her." Katrina charged forward like a bull in a china shop.

This dainty female had the gall to push at my chest, something not one of my brothers would ever attempt to do.

"I had little choice."

The little golden puppy sat on my booted foot and whined. The dog's amber eyes reminded me of Moira. I reached down, lifted the pup under his leg, and cradled him in the nook of my elbow. I'd fallen in love with Moira the moment she rejected me. She knew what she wanted and found the courage to stand up for what she believed.

Gabriel's words echoed in my memory. The journey to complete acceptance brings true enlightenment. My brother, always sentimental, saw the music in all aspects of life.,

The memory of that day when our archeias were separated from our bodies returned with cancerous anguish into our lives. I'd learned to handle the emptiness, and now I had to accept her rejection.

Each of my brothers handled the loss differently. By immersing myself in the justice system, I brought my light to those lost in darkness. Even after Father cast out Lucifer and Ananiel, I remained loyal. Suppressing the urge to rebel against everything I knew, I clenched my teeth together.

Once again, the pain rippled through me, and I didn't know if I could face the agony of loss. I knew that if I wanted to win her love; I had to risk my heart. I wanted to open myself, but the ironic twist was— I was afraid of losing.

How had Moira woven herself into my heart? I wanted to take her from Odin, and any others who could cause her harm. The frustration in my head mocked my usually logical lawyer's mind. The gems, the kundalini, were a chess game—a game of wits, knowledge, and skill.

My heart played little in the equation or outcome. As the thought struck me, Moira intended to end her life should she not survive the battle. I stiffened. She'd never allow her mother to use her to escape Odin's prison.

"Your face blanched a smoky shade of gray. Are you okay?" Lycre asked.

I looked at Brigit. "Moira's my spirit-mate; she carries the other half of my soul. If she dies, I'll lose my sanity."

Brigit tossed a fireball in my direction. "Capture the fire and you'll see Moira."

Without thinking, I gathered it in my palm, letting the fire absorb into my flesh. An ache filled me as brushes of trepidation touched my mind. Indecisiveness about what to do weighed heavily on my soul.

Visions of Moira flashed across my shields, screaming for me to pay attention. Two warriors raised their swords and, in unison, aimed for the back of her neck.

Telepathically, I reacted. "Dive underneath the largest man's legs."

Moira flew beneath the Viking in the nick of time.

With a wicked grin, I knew how to help her.

Brigit opened a gateway to her best friend.

I nodded.

She smiled.

"Form a circle, hold hands. We're going to Valhalla through mind transference," I said.

"Everyone, tap into the elemental magic of the earth." Katrina caught on to my plan.

I nodded as she tapped into each of our powers. Being an absorber, Katrina could enhance each of our skills. The power weave strengthened and opened the portal into Valhalla.

Lycre and the ravens' cunning insight into the home of the dead warriors helped us to navigate Valhalla and warn Moira of potential danger. The tendrils of our minds worked together to help her outwit the dead Vikings. I breathe a sigh of relief. We had broken no treaty rules, just side-tracked a few road bumps. My six wings expanded, along with Luc shielding our group in a protective circle. The Seraphim energy grew stronger, and in my angelic form I affixed onto the celestial energies of Kumuria. Using the golden light helped aid the circle against the dark magic that attempted to siphon Moira's mind while she fought the Viking warriors.

A warrior slashed his knife into her calf muscle, and Moira cried out and fell.

Gabriel and Rafael joined the circle and extended their wings. The four brothers worked through the blocked shields to help Moira feel their presence.

Katrina and Rafael healed her wound, giving Moira the ability to sprint away from the next attacker.

"Thanks," Moira responded.

My heart skipped a triple beat. Our strategy worked, and she recognized our presence.

"Behind you," Brigit warned.

Moira held the slave ring, now transformed into a sword, Silvercrest made for her as she let out a deadly war cry. She sliced the sword through the Vikings from gullet to breastbone.

He stood there, gaping mouth, then he toppled face down onto the grassy mound.

Moira cast a spell. "Lady of the mist, rise." Her arms rose like a conductor, bringing an orchestra to a final crescendo.

A misty mirage appeared before a group of Viking warriors, and a siren with long, flowing hair and creamy skin glistened there. She called the warriors by name. Panic rose in the men as they backed toward the edge of the illusory sea. Fear filled the men's eyes. When the siren placed her lips over the lad, he crumpled to his knees. "Come, be my lover and offer me your soul."

That got a snicker from the group.

Munin and Hugin laughed louder than the rest.

Every warrior dropped to his knees. The spell worked.

Odin appeared in our circle, ending the mind transference.

For a split second, I wanted for a second time to plunge him with my sword.

"Calm down." Munin grasped my arms.

Odin removed his helmet and met the gazes of Katrina, Brigit, Luc, Lycre, Munin, Hugin, Gabriel, Rafael, and me. "Your loyalty warrants the respect of the gods. Sarim prince. Your mate is a powerful witch, but she fears her own strength. Her confidence in her morality wanes. Complete the melding of your hearts, and she will see the glorious light."

Gabriel and Rafael closed their wings and gazed toward the vast emptiness of Valhalla.

"If you fail, we all will face the true death, never to regenerate as angels. That is the bargain made with Diablo." Rafael's smile was without humor.

Chapter Fifteen

MOIRA

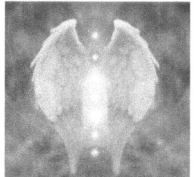

My body jerked as if I were falling out of the sky. My eyes fluttered open, my chest tightened, my heart pounded, and terror seized me. I gazed around and didn't recognize the room. "What happened?" I grabbed Uriel's arm, shoving aside the covers.

Uriel sat beside me, his fingers stroking my cheek. "Do you remember your ordeal with Odin?"

The battle in Valhalla came rushing back. Uriel and my friends helped me. "Where on earth was I?"

"In Lycre's house. You've slept for the past ten hours."

My father stood in the room's doorway. A sorrow of deep regret showed in the creases around his eyes. My heart wrenched at seeing his reluctance to enter the room. Shame flooded through me. I'd failed in my duties, and now he no longer wanted me. "Hi, Papa."

"Hello, Buttercup." His affection and despair radiated from the circle of light surrounding him.

My father, god of fertility and nature, never showed fear, but what he projected made me want to crawl under the covers and go back to sleep. "When did you arrive in Ventura?" Uriel stood and I slid from the bed, thankfully still wearing my leggings and tank top.

"I came with Katrina."

As if on cue, my two best friends came charging through the door and pushed me back onto the bed. The three of us talked all at once.

Next, angels and raven shifters filled the room.

Uriel's gaze was so galvanizing it sent a tremor through me. I craved to touch my fingers to his lips and tell him I missed him.

Lycre opened the sliding door that led out into the garden, letting in the fragrance of a barbecue. "Dinner's almost ready now that our warrior has awakened from her battle in Valhalla. Let's move this party from my bedroom and outside."

"Moira, we need to talk. I'll wait in the dining room." My papa turned and left the room.

"Ladies, my brothers and I could use your help in planning a wedding I'm sure we'll announce before long." Luc guided the women and the other shifters from the room, closing the door behind him.

Uriel didn't waste a minute before he was on the bed.

I opened my arms, and all thought ceased when he settled his mouth over mine. I drank deeply of his passion, wanting to thank him for not abandoning me in Valhalla. My heartbeat gained speed with each touch. His knee parted my legs, and I opened for him, feeling his hardness against me.

"I should have trusted us." I moved my hand down his buttocks, wanting him to heal the ache burning inside me.

He gazed into my eyes and softly murmured, "Mine."

I repeated the same word. "Mine."

As Uriel's eyes gleamed with fire, my insides soared with the heat of desire.

A soft tap sounded on the door.

"Time to join the others." I smiled, enjoying his attention. But my father and friends were in the next room.

"We'll be right out." Uriel kissed me and then rose from the bed.

Uriel helped me stand, and I went to the bathroom to freshen up. I returned to the bedroom.

Uriel sat in the corner chair, waiting.

I walked to the dining area where my father sat talking with a man whose identity hung on the edges of my memory. The individual with curly, wispy hair and the longest nose I'd ever seen took another slice of crumb cake.

Katrina gave him her sweetest honeybee smile. "Do you remember Loki? He's Hel's father. He's agreed to rescue Valefor from the pentagram."

Now I remembered. I hadn't seen him around since I was a child. "For what price?" Loki, a trickster god, didn't do favors for free. He'd expect payment in some form.

"I'm thinking of a lifetime of sweets made to my specifications." Loki stuffed a bite of the crumb cake into his mouth.

My life had taken a strange turn since the day Valefor stole the book and brought me into this nightmare. "Why are you helping us?"

"I have my reasons, but mostly, I owe your father a debt." He glanced at Freyr and smiled before he picked up his cake and went outside.

Uriel kissed me and followed Loki, closing the patio doors.

Freyr's long, bluish-black hair hung down his back in a single braid. As a little girl, I loved brushing his velvety hair while listening to his stories of wild adventures with the gods of the Vanir tribe. My favorite stories were his sailing adventures on his ship, the Skidbladnir. Once, I'd begged him to bring me along, and he'd taken out a pouch he carried and unfolded the ship before me. That afternoon, we rode through Alfheim, visiting all the coastal ports.

"Sit beside me, Buttercup. We have much to discuss."

Sadness washed over me. In the fridge, I found two Viking beers and poured them into icy mugs. Brigit brought a cranberry tart from the bakery, which I sliced for him. I set the refreshments on the table and placed a hand on my papa's shoulder. As the images flowed into me, I froze in a stunned tableau. His large hand cupped my wrist. "Papa."

"My torture is not for you to see."

I sat beside him, taking his hand in mine. "How did she capture you?" Tears brimmed my eyes as my repressed emotions tumbled out.

"During one of my voyages, Hel laid a trap for the silks and other cargo I carried. To release my ship and crew, she demanded I divert Odin's warriors from Valhalla to Niflheim. Hel prevented my leaving the underworld until I agreed to help. Years later, Hel learned of

Carman's treacherous use of the mare dreams to enslave my mind and body."

"Why didn't you tell me the truth about my birth?" My father flinched, regret searing his sorrowful expression. His eyes narrowed, and I felt him take an emotional step back.

"Did you know your name means fate?"

When I found my hands were shaking uncontrollably, my annoyance increased. I didn't want to hear how the gods manipulated people like expendable junk. "The gods play a cruel game with each other."

"I'm sorry."

"Sorry doesn't make me feel better. How do you think I feel knowing I'm spawned from an evil Celtic witch?" I stammered, wanting to blame him for my disgrace. Couldn't he have prevented my birth? Now, we all lived with the shame of who I was. I shifted my gaze to the floor, not wanting to see the disgust in his eyes.

His fingers lifted my chin, and his stern expression changed to softness. "Your blood is of my blood. Your flesh is of my flesh. You are more than a Seidr witch. You are the child of a god. I need you to renew and bring forth a new age. My daughter, you are the goddess who will bind every pantheon after the kundalini dragon rises within the galactic stars. Believe."

"And you're positive the light elves, the guardians, will defeat the dark elfin clans?"

"I have faith in you."

"Carman intends to resurrect on the eve of the blue moon during the priestess festival."

My voice revealed the bitterness brewing inside me. I wasn't a pawn. This conversation reminded me of a discussion Uriel and I had regarding the curse of the five Sarim princes. He'd felt betrayed. I understood his anger, so matched my own. "Papa, what if she escapes the underworld and enters the human world through me?"

He squeezed my hand tighter. "Do not focus your energy on Carman, but concentrate on what is true in your heart. For it is love that will save us."

"Are you saying, if I just fall in love, everything will go back to normal? No more war and no Carman?"

My father's laughter boomed throughout the room.

The sound made me relax and lean into him.

"I wish it were that easy. You and the other women must find their way back to their mates and together light the chakras of the kundalini dragon."

I wrapped my arms around my papa, relieved that I held a place deep in his heart. "I'm sorry you suffered so much."

He wiped his own tears. "I love you, my beautiful goddess."

For the first time since the ordeal with the grimoire books, I felt capable of handling just about anything. With my papa's words, my battle instincts stirred, my senses lifting to the next level of acuity. I'd stop Carman from hurting the people I loved.

Hand in hand, my father and I went to join the others outside.

Uriel touched my mind. "Everything okay?"

"My father says love will save us."

"He's partially right. Until you accept we're spirit-mates and become mine, the kundalini dragon can't rise."

Freyr released my hand. "Bring home the third book. The gem inside will decide the fate of our realm."

"Papa." I kissed his cheek, smiling.

"You and Uriel are the first spirit-mates. The Norn witches weave your story. Should you lose, we all lose."

A blood-curling scream came from Katrina.

Loki set Valefor, the duke of demons, on the ground in front of me, his body bloodied and drained.

A coldness of dark evil swirled around his etheric field, and I felt certain my childhood friend would die.

Baal's cruelty was unbearable, and I closed my eyes, fighting the impulse to flee from what lay at my feet.

Loki spoke to Brigit. "Take him to the demon realm. Yarrow is waiting."

Luc removed the infinity key from around Brigit's neck and placed it around his. "I'll take you." Lucifer picked up Valefor's body and walked to the edge of the yard where, with the key, he opened the doorway that bordered the demon realms, and they faded from human perception.

I turned back to the portal Loki had come through and stared at a man with the same features as myself. A knot of pure hatred gripped me. "Who's that?"

My father's face blanched. "Dother."

"Father and Sister. We meet at last." His voice bellowed as he straddled the otherworld portal. "Loki, you've won this round. Baal warns that if you re-enter his legions, he will sprawl and nail you to the pentagram.

I could feel a power rise in a silent battle of wills. Soon I'd make him pay for their crimes.

Papa moved toward Dother and faced him like the powerful king he was.

"You are unwelcome here. Alfheim is a realm of peace, ruled in harmony with the land. Stay in Niflheim, caged, hated spawn that you are."

Father advanced toward him and reached to pull him inside this realm. Dother blinked rapidly, and his chin quivered ever so slightly before he put his foot back into the portal. My father held power over him.

Dother's amber eyes turned cold. "Someday, I'll take your heart, seizing my rightful lands."

The metal of the slave ring, made with dwarf magic, vibrated, and I felt it pulling at Dother's powers. Deep inside, he felt the blackness of his mother's hatred. My father snatched my hand and covered it with his own.

"Do not allow the darkness to tarnish your soul. Dother's strength will weaken you and bind you to him. Odin has refused him access to the shifter territory. He is no threat for now."

The ring cooled, and Silvercrest's warning reminded me of the risk to my magic if I used the weapon in hate.

Katrina moved beside me and placed her hand over mine, pulling the remnants of Dother's magic from me.

Dother cocked his head toward her and smiled.

Being a channeler, her body consumed the dark magic I'd taken from him. Katrina collapsed to the ground.

Dother pulled her toward him, like a magnet drawing in metal.

I grabbed at her arms, but she vanished before my eyes. "Stop him from taking her!" my raspy voice screamed out in a hysterical cry.

My father and Uriel each grasped me to stop me from following him back to Niflheim.

"You can't go with her." Uriel pushed me into my father's arms. "Hold her."

"Let me go. Katrina needs me." I struggled against my father's forceful grip, trying to break free.

"Quiet, Buttercup." My father kissed my cheek. "We will go after her."

My tears burned like liquid fire. If Dother harmed my best friend, I'd kill him.

"Calm down," my papa murmured, letting me go.

I inhaled a ragged breath and went into Uriel's arms.

He kissed me and looked into my eyes. "We'll find her. I promise."

I stared down at a pool of dark red blood puddled where Valefor's body had been. With a foot, I touched Valefor's blood and recited, "Take this blood in sacred trust and vanish his pain into the earth." The blood disappeared. With gratitude, I gazed at Loki.

My father, along with Uriel's brothers, encircled me, allowing me a moment of privacy.

"The memory of you rescuing Katrina from the grasp of a family of ogres who kept her caged after she turned their youngest son into a toad is still vivid in my mind," my father said.

"He deserved it." Laughing at the memory of Katrina's outrage, I couldn't help myself.

"Dragging Katrina to the academy and demanding Freya enroll her in the same program as you and Brigit is something I remember." Freyr smiled.

Persuading my father took some wrangling, but after she took Freya's powers, it convinced Freyr of Katrina's use.

"She'll survive."

Uriel touched my arm, and for several surprised seconds I stared at him, feeling comforted in his confidence.

"Remember all the mischief the three of you got into?"

My father still continued to help me focus on the positive.

"We always succeeded." I reached for Uriel, and he wrapped his arm around my waist.

"You will this time, too. Stay connected in the triquetra of your friendship." Gabriel, Uriel's brother, took my hand. "You, Brigit, and Katrina are soul linked. The power of your relationship will protect the three of you in your time of need."

My gaze shifted towards my father. "I long for those carefree days when chasing goats and teasing Freya's cats were the highlights of my childhood."

"I miss those days. Those chocolate treats you always left in my office. I've yearned for them."

The nostalgia in my father's words warmed my heart. "I'll make you a basket of your favorites when this conflict is over."

My papa kissed my forehead. "I look forward to them. But now, it's time to accept who you are and embrace your Seidr skills of weaving destiny. The three Norns await your arrival."

Freyr and the others left me and Uriel alone.

Drained of emotions, I struggled to find the words I must speak. Instead, I reached up, and his lips touched me like a whisper stolen in the night. "Find Katrina, please."

His fingers caressed the hair on my face. "Trust me."

"I do."

Like no other, I desired him, but I held back. I didn't know whether I was ready for the commitment he demanded. No doubt, he'd expect a mate who loved him with every crumb of her life, but could he return the same love?

Hugin's caw told me it was time to go. I moved from Uriel's embrace and looked toward the sky. Munin and Hugin didn't give him a chance to say goodbye before a murder of ravens surrounded me with their outstretched wings, shadowing my body. Tendrils of magic pulled through every fiber as the birds transported me to Yggdrasil, where the three witches of the Norn sat weaving their web.

Chapter Sixteen

MOIRA

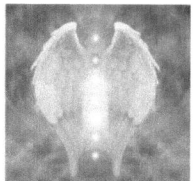

The ravens released me at the base of the world tree. I gazed over the lush foliage dotting the ribbons of green land. My sizzling emotions were in dreary contrast with the floating clouds that drifted over the prairie. My destiny overwhelmed me with these life-and-death responsibilities.

The image of my father chained to a stone slab, where he endured Carman's sexual perversions, was impossible to erase from my mind. I came into this world as the result of a violent and malicious act of rape, forever marked by the circumstances of my conception. I stroked my hands over my arms. My tainted flesh would never feel clean.

"Moira."

I froze and turned to face Urd, the oldest of the Norns.

In her weathered, gnarled fingers, she held a canvas with intricate patterns woven in various directions. Some paths stopped and ended, while other paths crossed over and continued. Three runic patterns paralleled each other before forking in another direction. Others held question marks, as if fate dangled freewill over humanity, waiting to see the outcome of their story.

The runes enchanted me, and I continued to read the story of the ages before the Great War. A time when humans and gods from many pantheons shared the skies, the earth, and the caverns. A time when the universe thrived in peace.

As she spun the thread on the canvas, Urd, the Norn of the past, clucked.

My story was being written. "What are you looking at, old woman?" I snapped, angry at the destruction of my life. I respected the three Norns and had prayed to them to help with the rewriting of destiny. But in my dark state of mind, I found the women troublesome.

"Pity is the worst sin. Continue, and you feed into the darkness threatening our land."

Knowing the woman was right, I sneered in frustration. "I don't feel sorry for myself."

"Sounds like pity." The woman continued with the spinning wheel in a soft, regulated tone.

"I'm tired of fate's cruel jokes. They're not funny." A distinct growl I didn't recognize erupted from my throat. "The three of you play with time. The witches toy with the gods, interfering in our lives. You keep the pantheons in chaos. The humans fear the magical realm because of you three.

But there's much you don't understand, even though you've studied history. Throughout the pantheons, our names vary. In Greek history, we are the Moirai, the goddesses of fate, and from whom you take your name. We are the mothers of life and the thread of every mortal from birth to death. We watch that the eternal laws of the gods may take their course without obstruction. Both God and man must submit to the universal plan."

A thunderous bellow sounded across the land. The clouds opened like curtains on a stage. The first original gods—Zeus, Solomon, Yahweh, Odin, and so many others—stood watching me.

I recognized the golden crown of thorns around Yahweh, identifying him as a god of the Celestial pantheon. I focused my desire on my slave ring. The dwarves' magic transformed the metal into a beautiful rope of silk, which lay in the palm of my hand. In a fraction of a second, I snapped the silk, and the cord encircled Yahweh's wrist. "Why did you betray your own sons?" I was determined to make him suffer for the cruel treatment of Uriel and his brothers.

Yahweh tugged on the rope, pulling me inches from him before speaking. "Mistress of fate, the key lies in your hands."

"Your heartless borders my mother's. Your son honors you. Yet, you watch them hurt."

An indefinable emotion sparked to life in his dark eyes.

"Don't judge what you don't understand, Moira, mother of light and dark."

His face taunted me as a round of memories filled me. The awful moment rose when my spirit split from Uriel. Thousands of years had passed since I'd held him close to my heart. My blood swelled with unbidden memories. "You are a merciless god to have made your own sons pay because of your failures."

"I will let your insolence go for now, for I agree my sons have endured far more than they should have. To resolve this dilemma, the three Norns of fate have offered the gods a challenge to rectify the wrong."

"I assume it deals with the kundalini?" I looked to Odin, the ruler of the Aesir Norse pantheon. Odin's one eye held a powerful wisdom for which he'd willingly paid. I trusted him, and I believed in my heart it was Odin who helped Freyr escape Carman's bondage.

"You are the strongest of the potential Seidr's. A lioness leader with so much courage. Your royalty line, combined with the Sarim prince, enhances your thought magic and the skill to harness the golden rays of the sun. You are the regal goddess, mother of protection."

Yahweh tugged at the silk of the slave ring. "During the challenge, many sacred and fallen angels from the nine celestial orders will help heal the conflict in my realm. The kundalini will bring together my sons and their archeia from around the other pantheons, reuniting and forming new bonds."

I couldn't release the hurt my soul still harbored at being forced out of the celestial realm and separated from my kindred spirit. "The curse has zero to do with the healing of Kumuria, but your own revenge at losing your wife in Diablo's realm. Your closed-mindedness in not understanding her inability to leave her two sons, whom you banished to the material realm, haunts you."

"Blasphemy," Yahweh snorted.

His cheeks colored a vibrant red, but I couldn't stop the rage pouring from me.

The three ancient Norns briskly wove a new pattern into the canvas.

My throat tightened, preventing the venom of my words from leaving my mouth.

"The daughter of destiny dances with light; daughter of destiny dances at night; daughter of destiny dances with earth," Verdandi, the fated norn of the present, sang while her fingers swiftly threaded the weave.

My gaze held Skuld's, the fate of the future, and I knew I must release the darkness blinding me to the light.

My heart screamed for Uriel, my kindred soul. Together, we were the muladhara, the root of the dragon chakra of the kundalini.

Fear held me back. My anger at Yahweh was justified, but my refusal to complete the bonding would condemn all the pantheons. I released the silk rope from Yahweh's wrist, determined to survive, to live, to fight, and to love. My slave ring returned to my hand.

Yahweh's cerulean eyes glistened with approval.

My hands moved of their own accord, drawing runic spells in the air to help vanquish the pattern of death.

Verdandi, with her seasoned fingers, created intricate patterns of darkness, death, war, and pestilence.

I worked even faster, challenging and contradicting spells, inserting magical weaves, and preventing the escape of those living in the underworld. If I allowed my mother's evil magic to dominate, I condemned the gods to relinquish control to the rulers of darkness. The anger in my mind slipped away as I fought to rewrite history and rewrite our destiny. I wanted to live. I wanted to feel Uriel beside me and to love him. My fingers wove an enchantment of oneness, giving in to my desire.

A golden light shimmered around Yggdrasil. Urd, the Norn of the past, stood with long curls hanging heavy over her shoulders. Thin tendrils of hair cupped the sunken flesh of her cheeks. A chortle came from her dry lips. "The past is who we are. The fate of time is never fair. It's a game and a challenge the gods have agreed to play."

The words of the Norn witches settled deep inside my heart. I'd always known our fates differed from humans. Maybe that's why I lived between the worlds of magic and humans. Now I'd be part of all the pantheons.

An awareness showered like beautiful crystals. My regression into the past flashed through my mind.

I cling to the roots of the world tree of the Norse nine worlds. My beloved home. After the severing of Uriel and my soul, I'd migrated to the elfin realm, living a multitude of lives. I looked at the images Urd weaved of my papa and saw his darkest pain.

The three Norns wove their hands over the present landscape, stitching blue and red threads into the fabric of time. A large, jagged split tore through the center, separating the halves. Fear crunched my heart. Dother used the spells of necromancy to siphon Uriel's strength. "Stop him."

Skuld wove new images of the future.

Dother opened a portal to the human realm and sent a gang of men to start a brutal bloodbath.

A knife sliced into Uriel's arm, leaving him vulnerable to his attackers. I screamed in terror.

As a celestial; he healed immediately, but with each blackened scar, the strength in his spirit grew darker. I feared for his life. Stop! I wanted to shout at Skuld, but her hands moved even faster.

"Dother intends to blacken his heart." Yahweh came to stand beside me.

Uriel's flaming sword plunged into one of the attackers' stomachs, pinning him to the ground. A howl filled my head, and I clasped my hands over my ears.

I turned toward the Norns. "Why do you create such horrid weaves?"

"Go to him. If Dother lives, Uriel will die, and the darkness wins." Verdandi spoke as more tears in the landscape rippled along the roots of the nine Nordic worlds. Skuld touched the Yggdrasil root. "Go before your archangel loses. The darkness claims the power it seeks."

My wrist's slave ring shivered, transforming into a cobalt lightning rod. The strength of light seized control.

Dother sliced open Uriel's back, severing part of his right top wing.

As I watched Dother kick him into the Aokigahara forest, a place where few returned.

My body twisted in agonizing pain, and I fell to my knees.

Yahweh's hand glided down my spine. "Save my son." He held the lightning rod over me. "Go."

"Mate." I jumped through the doorway to Svartalfheim, home of the dark elves.

Chapter Seventeen

MOIRA

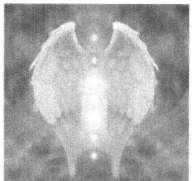

Deep in the underground tunnels of Svartalfheim, I sensed something was wrong as I climbed over the boulders and slid between crevices of jagged rocky land. Where were the sentinels who guarded the boundary walls?

A growl sounded in the void of nothingness, a flash of lightning, and suddenly, a lumbering, blood-stained, gray-blackish hound appeared. Two enraged eyes stared with debilitating severity. Another snarl came, and I hid behind the rock. Hiding was useless, since the hound's sense of smell would reveal my location. A misty fog rose along the border of rocks. A chill surrounded me, and I shivered, unable to stop the icy dread wrapping its tendrils around me.

The insistent bark of the hound grew closer. I retraced my steps, but found myself back in the exact spot I started. Emerging from the stones, Hel, Loki's daughter, walked towards me as the mist cleared. The soft touch of Hel's hound's nose against her hand made her smile. Standing at least three feet in height, the enormous animal had a colossal head that reached her waist.

As a child, I heard terrible rumors regarding her inability to escape Niflheim. A horrible curse burdened her, causing her body to be half alive and the other half decaying with death. I prepared to throw one of my knives.

She raised her staff and beckoned me to a halt.

"Welcome to the land of the living dead." Behind her, a sparkling castle opened into Niflheim.

Hel's beautiful, deep sapphire eyes with long, dark lashes bored into my own. I stopped myself from looking away. Instead, I focused on her shimmering locks of curly hair, not at the shriveling decay on the other side of her face.

I bowed in reverence to the queen of the dead, hoping to gain favor. If she'd gone to so much trouble to find me, she wanted something.

Hel's hand grazed my head. "Odin likes you. It behooves me to help you."

Odin offered his spear, and she handed me the weapon and an obsidian pebble. "Your Seraphim mate is a brave warrior. Fight for him. Use the spear once, then it will return to Odin."

I took the spear and used a glamour spell to hide it.

"Thank you."

"All the gods will eventually choose sides. During the challenge. Should any of the archeia angels face the true death, powers will shift."

"The Seraphim curse." Heat rushed to my cheeks, fearing the challenge we faced. Being the first archeia to reunite with my Sarim prince frightened me. I couldn't stop the adrenaline rushing through my system, making me want to hide within the safety of Sierra Madre, where the worst problem was dealing with a burned cake.

"You are the female soul of Uriel. The one to carry the light and save him. The kundalini must rise."

I guessed hiding was out of the question.

Hel turned and disappeared within her castle. The mist subsided as the portal gate to Niflheim closed.

I looked over the ridge along the border wall of Nidavellir and Svartalfheim. A sea of Aokigahara trees existed within the fork of the two territories. Still not sensing any soldiers, I reached the doorway leading into Nidavellir. A weave of powerful protection electrified the periphery. Did I risk entering the city? Instead, I sent a runic message to Dhubagret, who lived in the land of the dwarves. In the elfin forest.

Locate Silvercrest. Things are too quiet. Send a reply using our favorite rune.

No guards protected the gate surrounding Svartalfheim, which meant I surely walked into a trap. Using my telepathic sense, I caught a glimmer of Uriel's mind, but I couldn't connect with him. I settled between the rocks, waiting to be sure I wasn't walking into a trap before I continued into the ancient forest. Tiny cries floated in the air. A creepy feeling of dread surrounded me in all directions.

"Moira." A faint call.

"Katrina." I scanned the area around me and couldn't see signs of another person, but she was close.

"Moira, hurry. Uriel's hurt. Forest," Katrina gasped in raspy phrases.

"Are you alone?"

"Soldiers. She waits for you. Trap." Her words were weak.

"Where are you?" Terror clutched my chest.

"I'm alive. Save Uriel. Dother."

Her words faded.

Katrina's tiny body wouldn't survive an overload of magic without a way to release the excessive energy. And if Dother tortured her, I'd kill him. I continued over the ridge in front of me.

A wild dog with gray eyes stared with a bone-chilling intensity, a battle cry resonating from its ghastly mouth.

Ready to kill the beast, I raised Odin's spear. Using a teleporting ball, I materialized at the forest's border, giving the dog a wide berth.

I needed to slow my heart and catch my breath. Forcing my legs to stand, I stepped through the magical doorway, which opened to a woodland of intertwined trees with spiny tendrils of limbs. I surveyed the area, still waiting for the sentinels I knew should be present. I moved forward and bounced back. A wall of magic protected the entrance into the forest, which explained the lack of guards. Katrina was here somewhere. I could hear her soft whimper of pain.

Reaching inside my boot, I pulled out my knife and prepared for an attack. I studied the weave and deciphered its pattern. Consiortus increorgio. A light ruby stream swirled within the patterns, revealing the magical auras of anyone hidden within the weave.

Katrina screamed.

I turned toward her voice. Before me, her two-inch pixie body stared back. They wove her into the spell. "What have they done to you?"

Katrina absorbed the magic within the web, causing her to writhe in pain.

When I touched the weave, I winced as her body spasmed. Unshed tears blurred my vision while the sorrow closed my throat. My hands wove quickly and created a healing shield over Katrina. When she opened her pixie eyes, relief flooded through me. Her small wings fluttered within the invisible veil.

"Estiior Padlaris. I've created a skin-like barrier of frosty energy. Hang on." I double-checked the pattern and sealed it the best I could. "Better?"

"Go to Uriel; he's bleeding."

"Where is he?"

"On this side of the wall."

I walked the length of the doorway, but the magic barrier barred my entrance. In the far corner, I found him. Below, in the sea of trees, Uriel lay unconscious on his stomach.

"Welcome, daughter."

My mother stood before me.

"I knew you'd come for your little friend."

"What do you want?"

"Bring me the jewel embedded in the grimoire's third text."

"I don't know where it is." Nobody's signature resonated from her. I charged toward her, and nothing happened. An illusion spell. I turned, catching a drift of a scent. Elfin.

King Hagmer stepped from beyond the trees with his soldiers of dark elves behind him. Carman's energy flashed in and out, the spell losing its strength.

Hagmer's finger pierced Katrina right under her wing. "Bring the book, or I'll slice her wings to shreds."

"Leave her alone." Swirls of particles wove through my hands as I focused on the maroon energy enforcing the protective barrier around Katrina. Blinded with rage, I poured my anger into the slave ring and stole the life force from the warriors standing behind their king.

One by one, the men fell to their knees.

I incapacitated his army. I had little time to unravel the barrier and get us out of here.

Carman's eyes widened with a steely, haughty glare. "You are a powerful Seidr. A loyal daughter of my spirit."

Her magic weaved around my aura, and the darkness consumed my light, turning me into the evil I hated. I fought to take control of the slave ring. "Firergio Tyreris. Restore the souls to their bodies." If I killed them, I'd become my mother's perfect weapon.

As the etheric spirits returned to his men, Hagmer raised his weapon. "Carman, stop. If one soldier dies here, the blood will be on your hands, and they will bind you for another thousand years."

A blast of intense repulsion hit the middle of my chest. After the last of the spirits returned, I slammed against the ground. Breathless, I lay spent, unable to move.

Carman's tall, regal form stood over me like a goddess of perfection. Her beauty was so out of place for one so evil.

"I enjoyed tasting your anger. The emotion feeds me and nourishes my soul. But our day will come when I take what is rightfully mine, and nothing you do will reverse the darkness dwelling within your soul."

I crawled to my knees and resisted with all my might not to cry out in pain. "You will not gain one stronghold in the light elfin province." Carman's laughter echoed throughout the hills. I struggled against the excruciating pain in my head.

"Bring me the book, or the pixie dies."

I lifted my chin and fought the nausea threatening the back of my throat. Not giving in to her power, I met her icy gaze. "If you kill Katrina, I promise you will burn in the worst hells of Muspelheim." I watched the coldness in her eyes before she nodded to one of the dark elves.

He lifted my limp body.

Pain rippled through every fiber of me.

"Bring me the map of the ley lines and the gem, or the pixie suffers the loss of her wings." The soldier tossed me toward the sea of trees.

My body landed beside Uriel in a pile of contorted roots. Another thud sounded beside me, and Odin's spear lodged in the branches of the fir tree.

Chapter Eighteen

URIEL

I woke with a throbbing pain in my first wing. Gathering my strength, I braced my hands on the ground and pushed to a sitting position. A stabbing pain jolted up my spine, shoulder blades, and out my wings. I remember I'd located Dother within the Aokigahara forest. I'd released my wings and intended to enter from the sky. When I hovered above the trees, soldiers attacked. Holy shit, my mouth tasted rancid. My head spun worse than after a good binge of Scotch. Clearing my thoughts, the first thing I needed was to heal my wing and find a way out of here.

A whimpering moan registered in my foggy brain. I looked around to see Moira's body lying at a strange angle. What was she doing here? The last time I'd seen her, the ravens were taking her to Yggdrasil to meet with the fates of Norn. With grief in my heart, I closed my eyes and fought the emotion. I knew she'd searched and tried to save my life.

As the tendons of my wing fused together, sweat broke out on my brow, and my muscles trembled like a newborn baby. I dry-heaved as the first of the pain subsided. On my hands and knees, I did a complete scan of my torso. No other wounds.

I saw Moira about a hundred feet to my right. I inched my way to her and moved my hands over her body. They broke her arm. I could heal the bones, but she'd feel the agony of every cell as it repaired itself.

"Uriel." Her sweet voice called to me.

"Don't move. Your arm's broken."

Moira leaned on her other elbow and instantly fell back to the ground. "Fudge brownie sticks, my arm really hurts."

"This isn't the fudge with the amnesia potion, is it?" I wanted to distract her from the pain.

"I'd love a dose right now," she moaned, and a quick gasp of air came from her chest.

"If you have any pain-distracting spells, conjure them. The bone will hurt as it mends." I held the radius, thankfully a clean break with no shattered bone fragments. Warmth flowed through my hands like an electrical charge. All angels carried the ability to heal, but using it drained their sensory awareness. I'd be a sitting duck if attacked, unable to defend or protect Moira. I felt little choice over sacrificing the energy. If her broken arm mended incorrectly, she'd lose her ability to wield her knife, leaving her vulnerable to attack.

"Sweet lemon cakes, I'll skin you alive."

Purple shadows formed beneath her eyes, a sure sign of the agony she experienced. Once the pain subsided, her arm would heal quickly. The tension in my shoulders relaxed. She was fine if her thoughts were about baking. "In fact, I could use an enchanted buttercream vanilla cake. Do you have any food in your pack?"

Moira rolled her eyes and leaned back into the bed of leaves. Her color turned a warm glow of pink instead of the ashen gray. "I strapped a few blueberry protein bars to my leg inside my boot."

I was kidding about the food, but I needed nourishment, and by the looks of Moira, she did, too. I moved a hand underneath her leggings, wanting to feel the soft warmth of her velvety skin. My resolve to keep my distance faded. We were mates, and time was running out. Strapped to her calf, I found four bars alongside three packets of potions. The woman was her own apothecary. I unwrapped one bar and handed it to her.

Her golden eyes glistened with tears. "What can I do?" I rubbed my knuckles along her cheek.

"Carman has Katrina. Hagmer is torturing her."

Her gaze clung to mine. "What do they want?" I kissed her temple and held her tight in my arms.

"The book of ley line maps and the gem." Her head dropped to my chest.

As I pieced together the dilemma, a sick knot of tension tightened in my gut. How could I choose who to save?

Using telepathy, Skuld knocked on my shield. "May I speak?"

"I am listening."

As Skuld's words warned me of the future, Moira's fingers massaged the scar under my breastbone.

"Mate with her and join your strengths. Profess your love to each other. Hurry! Do not tarry. Hagmer intends to invade Freyr's lands while Moira deals with her mother."

"Your words don't inspire lovemaking."

"Make her yours, for many lives depend upon your bond."

"You're miles away." Moira touched my hand.

Her amber eyes filled with concern; a softness drew me, and I wanted to get lost in their depths. People reveled in the sweet fragrance of hope and dreams her baking provided. She offered the promise of a brighter tomorrow. Only now did I see her true beauty and her real purpose. I kissed her softly on the forehead. This woman would be my wife, my mate, and my lover.

"We'll rescue Katrina."

"I'm scared."

I nuzzled her neck, soaking in the vanilla scent. Her fragrance was soft honey, drawing me like a bee to its source. I sucked her tongue into my mouth and exerted a more provocative pressure. My senses reeled as if short-circuited. The fire of passion grew like I hadn't felt in eons.

She ran her fingers along my jawline. "The flame dances in your eyes."

"And in yours." The yellow flame burned with a wildness I couldn't wait to explore.

The tenderness I'd long forgotten. Ages had passed since I'd enjoyed just a kiss. Usually, with women, sex was savage and fast and forgotten. The slowness enticed me, making my blood pound in my brain. But lovemaking had to wait.

Chapter Nineteen

MOIRA

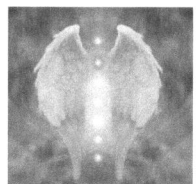

My body trembled under the slowness of Uriel's kiss. Nothing in my life ever felt this good or this right. The voice of fate rang in my ears. He is your destiny. The Norn witches infused me with the knowledge of my fate. Their words sang in my heart as Uriel's hot mouth moved down and across my throat.

Weariness filled me, but the more he kissed me, the more strength I regained. "Make your eyes dance with fire for me."

"Anything, cupcake."

The fire blazed in his eyes, and I understood its meaning. No longer afraid of what it meant, I eagerly wanted him inside of me. Not in a million lifetimes again would I push him away. "I need you, my spirit-mate." The words, like chocolate, tasted good.

"How's the arm?"

"Stronger." I moved away, surprised at how quickly I'd recovered. The menacing residue of dark magic left my body, enabling me to feed off the light and restore equilibrium in my mind. Heat flared in Uriel's eyes, and my own internal flame burned with satisfaction.

"Moira," he whispered.

His mouth found mine, and our tongues danced together in a silent melody. A tickle pricked at my ankle. Not wanting to end the kiss, I used my other foot to scratch at the itch. I placed my hands on his chest and pulled away. "Something's wrong." I looked at my feet and screamed. Green vines wrapped around my ankles. I stiffened and tried to move, causing the vines to tighten their grip.

"Are any of the potions strapped to your leg capable of helping us out of here?" He sat up and pulled me into a sitting position. "We're not alone, and the elfin forest has secrets."

I reached into my fanny pack and searched for a teleporting ball. "Where to?"

Uriel grasped my waist and gave me a quick kiss. "To Narusawa Village."

I wrapped my arms around Uriel and visualized the quaint village nestled close to the caverns. I squeezed the ball, and we materialized in a section of conifer and broadleaf trees. In this part of the world, the magical realm stayed deeply embedded within the forest and caves. Mount Fuji was a favorite place for the dwarves, with hundreds of volcanic lava tubes interconnecting the human and magical realms. "What's the plan?"

"Hot shower, sex, and food."

"We don't have time for those luxuries. Carman's holding Katrina hostage."

"That's exactly why we're getting a room, taking a shower, and creating a game plan."

The delay was not ideal, yet I needed time to stop Carman from getting the book. I approached a Japanese lodge surrounded by a running stream and onyx rocks for meditating. The design unexpectedly resembled square boxes with sliding roofs that overhung the exterior siding. Outside the lobby door, a basket full of pine cones from the conifer trees gave off a decomposing odor that irritated my nose.

Uriel dangled a key from his fingers. "This is our lucky day, and cabin twelve is available. The room at the far end of the street."

Being at the end of the lodge gave us a semblance of privacy. I entered the cabin. Uriel tossed the key onto the table. "I'll take a shower first, then order dinner while you clean up."

"Sounds good." While sitting on the bed, I could feel the weight of rescuing Katrina seep into my aching muscles. Contacting Dhubagret is necessary to inform her of the change in plans. I still needed her and Silvercrest's help. Since Nidavellir bordered the Nordic side of the forest, I should be able to send a rune through the veils. I drew a quick message in the air, telling her to meet me in the ice caves where she'd hidden the third book. Swirling a journey spell around the runes, I opened the door and visualized Silvercrest's, where I assumed Dhubagret was staying. At dusk, Uriel and I would need to hike to the ice cave without drawing the attention of any tourists. I crossed my fingers and prayed to Odin that Dhubagret would be there to help.

Chapter Twenty

URIEL

I'd laid out a variety of sushi rolls, yellowtail, and soup. The shower turned off. "Moira, the food's ready."

"I'll be out in a minute."

She'd grown quiet, and her extreme silence cautioned me that trusting her to give me the gem, instead of Carman, might prove to be the hardest trial in my life. Moira, my spirit-mate, had to choose to take her place as the priestess of the kundalini, mother goddess of hope for the other four angels.

The bathroom door opened onto an amber glow of energy. Her elfin essence overshadowed the insecurities creeping into my mind. "You're beautiful."

She appeared different, sure of herself. She reached for me, and for several surprised seconds I stared, unsure of my next move.

"I know what I want."

Her wet hair kinked into tiny curls, enticing me like no other female. I fought back the insane desire to pull her close and make her understand the need within my soul. Her lips touched mine in a tender caress, and my body weakened. In utter bliss, I lifted her in my arms and laid my mouth on hers. The kiss was sweeter than the nectar used in her cakes. Every scent of her smelled of vanilla. "Look at me."

She did.

The same fiery flames danced in her eyes with a heart-rending tenderness that told me she was ready to become my mate.

"Why are you still dressed?" She let the towel drift, revealing one of her breasts.

A rush of desire that clawed and clutched at my insides was a powder keg ready to blow. I blew hot air against her pale-rose nipple before taking it in my mouth. A low moan slipped past her lips. A husky, helpless sound of want escaped Moira, and my cock hardened, anticipating having her.

Her fingers traced up my zipper, caught the tab, and drew the zipper down. I needed her to wrap those sexy fingers around my cock and fuck me with her hand.

As if reading my mind, she squeezed the base and pumped. I stroked her breast, enjoying the view. Taking me completely off guard, she pushed the flap of my jeans and took me in her mouth, running her tongue over the thick vein on the underbelly of my shaft.

I couldn't take much more of her teasing before I blasted a load, and that was not how I wanted our first time to be. Pulling my cock from her sweet mouth, I found my breath and removed my jeans.

She lay on the bed with one knee bent and her hands on her abdomen.

Sweet angels, she was beautiful, with her pink pussy staring at me.

"Touch yourself. I want to watch and learn what you like." Elves were passionate lovers, and Moira would be the sweetest of cream. As I watched her slide her hand over her luscious mound of red curls, I ran my tongue over my bottom lip.

"You like to watch?"

Her fingers slid along her thigh, drawing my eye to the very pot of honey I'd been dying to taste for days. I'd let her play for a moment longer, then I'd join her. "Put your finger inside. Seeing the juice flow from your body is what I want. I watched in bliss as one finger, then two, dipped into her wet pussy. Her arousal was clear, intensifying my response. Before I tasted her, I wanted her wet and begging for me.

"I'm coming."

"Come for me, baby. Let me see your lips tighten against your fingers." She screamed my name, and that's when my mouth covered her pussy, replacing her fingers with my tongue.

"Oh, holy shit."

She bucked against my mouth.

I closed my hands over her hips, holding her still. I wasn't close to being sated and still feasted. "Again, my sweet."

"I can't." Her fingernails dug into my shoulders.

My consciousness ebbed and then flamed, the spirit-mating melding. Her mind and spirit called to me, giving me all of herself.

I found her entrance, and both our shields faded as we blended as one, coming together in the true meaning of the one soul. My archeia had returned home. My emotions whirled and skidded as pleasure radiated outward, and I released my body, mind, and soul into Moira, my archeia.

Still gasping for air, I caressed her cheek. "Flesh against flesh, man against woman. Never again will we separate." Never had I felt such warmth and contentment. As I cradled Moira with my body, I held her close and reveled in the feel of her. "I love you."

"You are the missing piece that completes my day," he admitted, his eyes filled with love. "Your heart beating reverberates in my ears, a constant reminder of your presence."

"As I do yours. Our souls have returned to one another."

Both cell phones rang.

"What do you want to bet the texts from Brigit and Luc?" Moira laughed as we turned to the table where our phones lay.

I picked up my phone and opened Messages. A picture of a dragon formed in the clouds. The dragon kundalini is flying high in the skies, telling the world you've mated. Awesome brother.

I texted back, Still have to locate the jasper stone and complete the task.

Text: I have faith in the two of you. Brigit wants to know if you've found Katrina.

Text: Hagmer has her.

Text: Be careful, I'm heading back to Kumuria and then Alfheim to check on Valefor.

"I'm afraid." Moira's cheek rested on my chest.

I tightened my arms around her, never wanting her to be scared.

"What if you die? I don't think I could survive."

Her voice rang with panic and trembled with fear. "You would. No matter what lifetime we live in, we'll always find each other."

"You sound so certain."

I kissed her tenderly, feeling whole. "I am my love, my life, and my soul. You are forever my mate." I held her close, fearing my words were a lie. The true death would turn us to dust, separating our souls for all time.

"We're in more danger because of Carman and Diablo, aren't we?"

"Until we return the red jasper stone to the Muladhara chakra, those who desire the dark to rise will attempt to thwart our goal."

"The curse didn't feel real until now."

"The destiny of millions lies upon our shoulders." I wrapped my arms tightly around the woman I loved, for tomorrow could be the day of the true death.

Chapter Twenty-One

MOIRA

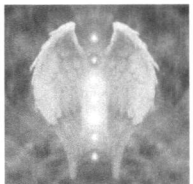

The next evening, we prepared to retrieve the gem from its hiding place. "Strap Odin's spear to my back." I scanned the lodge for my fanny pack. Now that we'd reconnected our souls, I feared the loss of him. I wouldn't survive, should any of the dark elves caused him harm. The bond, if severed, would destroy me. I'd never return to baking, because I would lose my heart in the depths of despair. My soul, intertwined with his, felt like being one person.

"Quit fretting."

"I'm not fretting."

"What's all that chatter going on in your head? You're giving me a headache."

I reached up and kissed his mouth. Now that we'd let down the walls, personal space lost its meaning, and I felt the urgency to touch him. Uriel sensed my stress and rubbed his knuckles down my cheek in a possessive gesture that let me know I was his and only his.

"What did the rune message say?"

"Dhubagret's meeting us at the entrance of Narusawa ice caves, then we'll rescue Katrina from the spider web of woven magic that connects the elementals together."

I strapped my knives onto my calf and put on the slave ring, making sure it could easily slip from my wrist if they attacked us. Next, I added the last of my potions.

"I called for a rental car, and a taxi's waiting at the front office to give us a ride to town." Uriel put his arms around me. A devilish look came into his eyes. "We'll come back here every year and celebrate our mating."

"Such a romantic." My whole body throbbed with the need for this man to keep me forever in his arms.

"I'm completely in love with the most beautiful priestess in the world." A peaceful smile played at the corners of his mouth.

"You keep talking with endearments and when we get home, I'll bake you as many cakes as you like."

"Promises."

He kissed the pulsing hollow at the base of my throat, sending hot arrows to my core. "We have to go."

His lips left my neck.

"Create an invisibility spell around our weapons and tone down your elfin features. You're glowing with the sparkle of a woman well-loved."

"I've shielded us both with elfin glamour. Are you ready to go?"

I stepped outside into a cauldron of fiery crimson purples, absolutely a sight to take away one's breath.

If anyone saw us on the human side of the Japanese forest, we'd look like traditional American tourists. I was grateful he didn't have an excessive need to talk on the twenty-mile drive. I mentally rechecked my knives and spells. What would we do if any of the dark elves intercepted and deciphered the runic message? My stomach churned, half-expecting Carman to appear and foil our plans.

Uriel reached for my hand and squeezed.

All his love came pouring inside of me.

He parked outside the gate of the rear structure.

The last of the tourists were leaving, so we shouldn't draw too much attention.

I pressed a palm to my heart and uttered a whisper of gratitude. Dhubagret sat on a boulder underneath a patch of trees in a purple denim jacket, wrapped in many scarves and gloves. "So, it's true."

"What's true?"

"You're radiating an amber light hidden beneath the glamour. The swirling energy stimulates everything around you."

My cheeks flushed hot enough to melt ice. Uriel's strength surged through my system, making my own powers increase in effectiveness. Colors illuminated with remarkable, amplified vibrancy. I missed the bakery, where I could make brownies with sparkles, the warmth of the oven a contrast to the feelings that coursed through me.

"Silvercrest sends his congratulations and promises to make your wedding bands."

"Does everyone know we've mated?" A flush burned my cheeks, remembering how our bodies came together in that perfect union.

"Well, those in the realm of magic can't help but see the dragon. The red energy is swarming throughout the horizon." She reached her hands in the air, and a powerful gust of wind whipped tree limbs into a riotous dance of tangled branches. "Just look at the sunset. Its rich energy blazes in all the pantheons. Even the dwarves have climbed above ground to witness the consummation of seraphim and Aesir, both children of the gods."

Uriel waved at Dhubagret right as I jumped into her arms, overwhelmed with all the excitement reflected in her eyes.

"I couldn't be happier, except that Katrina's being held captive."

"What will you do?"

I tilted my head and looked into Dhubagret's eyes. "Seems to be the million-dollar question. I'm too far away to locate her telepathically. And I've no clue whether Freya can rescue her."

The three of us waited until security locked the gate.

Once the parking area emptied, we climbed over the fence and followed the bamboo stairwell to the cave's entrance. The book rested in the lava tube closest to the Aokigahara forest and the doorway into Nidavellir, where dwarf soldiers protected the border. We had little time before nightfall blanketed the mountain. Using the human realm to enter the caves instead of the Nordic portal gave me an opportunity to avoid the dark elves and hopefully retrieve the book undetected.

Uriel handed Dhubagret and me hard hats from a large crate at the gate. "Put these on before you start the descent down the stairs."

Once inside, I used one of the illuminating potion balls to brighten the room and guide us to the pool of a triangular crystal formation that resembled the ancient runic symbol of the dragon's eye. The water curved like a coiled snake. The deeper I went, the light cast a radiant indigo over the shimmering ice like a cold fountain of blueberries.

"Underneath the second ridge, you'll find an ancient silver crystal case filled with the powers of our ancestors. I placed the book inside, knowing the ancestral spirits would protect the grimoire. I've encircled it with an outer plain vessel containing a contagion potion." Dhubagret motioned toward the small opening.

Studying the pattern, I quickly released the wards protecting the book and lifted the antique from its hidden safe spot.

"Don't open it here. Wait until you're positive no one will attempt to steal it. Here's the neutralizer."

The tin case holding the book barely fit in my backpack.

"We need to go." Uriel gave Dhubagret a hug.

I turned to my good friend, not knowing how I could repay her for risking her life to help me. "I'm so sorry for your shop and for endangering you in the elfin battles."

"Go on. Silvercrest is waiting." Dhubagret's gaze darted toward the portal. Then she grasped my hands. "He's asked me to marry him."

I squeezed. "And?"

"I've said yes."

"I will make the perfect wedding cake for you."

Silvercrest stood in the otherworld portal, signaling to Dhubagret to leave the dangers of the ice cave and return to the safety of Nidavellir.

"I'm safe. Now go. Katrina needs you. Go."

Tears fluttered at the tips of my eyelashes. I embraced her close. "Thank you."

"Hurry." Dhubagret disappeared into the crevice and into Silvercrest's arms. I hoped no one was waiting to ambush them once they made it through the doorway.

Uriel's hand clasped onto mine. "Ready?"

"Yes." I climbed the stairs in the dark, not taking any chances that the illuminating spells would signal our presence. The explosion of ice behind me startled me, and I nearly stumbled, worried Dother or

Carman might be on our heels. Their failure to decipher the runic code suggested an inherent vulnerability.

"Relax, the sound is of the ice calving."

I held tightly to Uriel's hand. I had to get to the border between the otherworld and make sure Katrina was safe. After leaving the ice cave, Uriel drove the car back to the hotel. I went inside, grabbed a couple bottles of water. Uriel left the rental keys on the table, just in case we didn't make it back.

As I made my way through the Aokigahara lodge trail, the foliage grew thick with vines.

"Over here. The doorway is to the right."

A mossy patch of rocks covered the entrance. I touched my finger to the portal opening to sense if sorcerer magic surrounded the passageway. The magic here was old.

Uriel went first.

I followed and emerged into the blinding sunshine of the Nordic realm.

Katrina's weak body dangled from the spell web that swayed between the human and Nordic otherworld doorways. Bruises and sunburn marked her extremities; her lips were dry, and her eyelids had swollen shut.

I fought the nausea burning in my throat. Using a leaf, I gave her water.

"Help me!" Katrina's tiny voice whimpered.

My throat parched with clogged tears, I was afraid I could hurt her if I tugged or pulled the wrong way. "I risk killing you if the unraveling spell fails."

Her raspy voice cried out in pain, "Take me home." Katrina coughed as her head leaned against the web, and no other sound came from her.

I pulled on the magical energy from the muladhara root of the earth's power. Our magic fused. Panic still welled inside me, fearing I could kill my best friend.

I closed my eyes, refusing to succumb to my insecurities. "Uriel," I yelled. "Carman's power is too strong. I need your help."

The jolt of earth power that shoved into me caused me to stumble. I had to mix his strength with mine to gain control and use the magic.

"Concentrate."

Falling to my knees, I pushed back at Carman's hold. One of Katrina's legs became free.

"How are you doing?"

"Almost figured out the signature pattern, just a few minutes more and she should be free." Without warning, a power punch whipped me through the air, crashing me against the magical barrier. Dother and the dark elves rushed toward the border and right for me. "Get the spear. It's strapped on my back," I screamed with every ounce of emotion left in me.

"Hurry, my love." Uriel took Odin's spear and angled it toward Dother.

On my knees, I crawled to the outer knots of the web. Thousands of complicated patterns crisscrossed in my mind's eye. There it was—the base of the pattern. With a confident smile, I continued to unravel the weave and more of her body hung free.

The last layer, and then I saw it. The core of the spell, a colorful rope of thick golden thread woven around Katrina's wrist. "I did it." The weave untangled, and her tiny body dropped into my hand.

"Fucking hurts," her scratchy voice whimpered.

The web disappeared. Dwarven soldiers from Nidavellir galloped toward the dark elves, and all hell broke loose.

Uriel, on a large stallion, chased one of my brothers. "What in fudge cakes?"

In Celtic armor, a silver rope grasped me around my arms, pinning them against my body. My brother tossed me over the horse's saddle in front of him and leaped into Svartalfheim.

Katrina fell from my hand.

"Uriel!"

Color drained from Uriel's face.

Chapter Twenty-Two

MOIRA

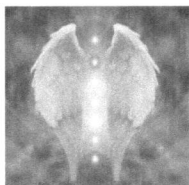

Inside Svartalfheim, the fighting sounded so far away, and all I could see were sharp, protruding rocks as my head swung upside down. I buried my face in the horse's side to prevent the dust and rocks from pummeling me. We entered the otherworld pathways, and a chilly feeling crept around me when another portal closed behind my brother and me. Once he slowed; I kicked my feet, trying to dislodge his hold. "Holy fudge sticks, let me off this horse."

Instead, his hand came down hard on my bottom. I yelped, not expecting the tingling sharpness. A cold gust of wind and a spray of rain whipped over me. I stared at the ice forming on the ground. Where were we? The dark, moonless night was devoid of stars. A chill filled me. We stopped, and he grabbed a handful of my hair, yanking me into a sitting position.

"I will put a knife in your gut," I hissed, struggling to free myself.

"Little sister, welcome home to Niflheim."

His hot breath touched my ear.

I swallowed hard. A cold, clammy sweat broke out on my body, and the hair on the back of my neck spiked. I had no chance against Carman if my spells were useless.

As we continued along the roadway, a ghostly group of people exited decrepit structures. A siege of sadness overwhelmed me at the desolate lack of joy within these people. Most stared with emptiness in their eyes.

The horse slowed to an even trot. Magical wards around the arched walkways kept the weeping shackled in the quads, awaiting their judgment. Wards of complexity overwhelmed most of the lost elves or dwarves of the Nordic pantheon, who found themselves in Niflheim, the land of the unworthy dead. Escape was impossible.

In the center of Hel's realm, the lowest of Yggdrasil roots twisted in massive, gnarled knots. My abductor rode through the town until he reached a moat that encircled the first layer of sadness. The next level was misery.

I had no intention of going past this mark. I kicked the horse's underbelly, forcing him to buck.

The rider's hand clamped over the saddle-horn and the other held the reins. He brought the horse under control.

"Nice try."

My captor dismounted. His large hands grasped my waist, and he lifted me off the stallion. An uncomfortable ache surged through my muscles as I continued to wiggle my hands free.

In front of an overarching bridge that opened into a vast expanse of despondent communities, Carman stood holding a blue shield with wrapping patterns of Celtic knots on a black background depicting her Fomorian crest.

A plan formed in my mind. The bridge descended into the third level of regret. I'd studied the book of necromancers and understood how Odin kept her prisoner. That's why she needed the gem and the map of the otherworld pantheons. My mother lived in the dead world. She could only project her image, the very picture I'd seen at the borders between the dark elfin and dwarven lands. In the distance, thousands kneeled on bended knees.

Two men stood behind her.

I recognized Dother. I fought the ache to use my slave ring and stab a sword into his dark heart.

The other man radiated such an ominous cloud that I recoiled at the shadows flowing from his body.

My captor untied my wrists, but before I could reach for my knife, an iron grip pressed in close, and steel ropes of magic wrapped around my torso.

"Welcome home, little sister." Dother walked over the bridge and lowered his mouth to mine.

The act was so vile I gagged and kicked.

"Ah, little one, I've watched you in town and spied on you with your friends. Thought about the day I'd bring you home."

My jaw tightened. His breath, hot on my skin, made my nostrils flare. I spat in his face. "Stay away."

His hand clenched my throat.

My lungs felt like they'd burst from lack of oxygen. I struggled to make a choking noise that sounded like something out of a dying animal.

"Enough."

Carman called him off like the dog he was.

"Bring her to me."

He released me. I barely caught my breath before my abductor yanked my hair and dragged me toward the bridge.

"Dereseos Arundis." I called on Valefor and his legions of demonic energy to rise and fight with me. "Take your vengeance against Dother," I commanded.

"Valefor lacks power. Hagmer still rules his legions. Did you know, little sister, I played with his soul before Loki found him bloody and dying? Call on your friend. He served me well," Dother said.

My heart ached at the treatment he'd experienced because of me. "You will burn in Muspelheim, where every demon will pluck out your eyes and watch you bleed."

Carman's tawny eyes narrowed to yellow slits. A sardonic laugh tore from her like a whirl of icy wind. "Odin's gods will pay with the destruction of his pantheon for leaving me to rot in the coldness year after year."

Her words were frigid as she turned her fury on me. I struggled against my captor's restraints, my magic paralyzed.

"You are the revenge I seek. We will take back what is ours and rule with the dark ones. Daughter, you will be by my side."

The idea made my stomach retch. I'd never stand with her, even to save my life. Each of my brothers' yellow eyes reflected the darkness within their souls.

Odin, please let it be true that no evil lives in my blood. "What do you want, Carman?" I refused to call her mother and give her that honor in my life.

"Hand over the secret of the Norns."

"Why do you want it?" I had to stall her until I could figure a new game plan.

"When I sent you to live with the Nordic gods, I knew you'd return, and you have. Now, give me the book." Carman extended her hand.

"Your own gods disowned you. They left you to rot for the crimes against the Fomorian Irish people. The Tuatha De Danann rejoice in your suffering."

The man kicked my lower back.

I stumbled onto the bridge. Anger surged through me, and I refused to cower. I rose in dignity and turned toward my brother with desperation in my mind. "Why do you stay here when you can leave? Odin doesn't hold you prisoner."

"We've aligned with the dark elfin clan. Our home is in Svartalfheim, and we're members of the royal courts of Hagmer."

I wasn't sure if this was Dain, the one known for violence, or Dub, the evilest of the three. I'd take a chance and see if I guessed right, and Dain took the bait.

Your royalty, son of a god. Why play second to a ruler who only dreams of Freyr's power? Freyr will give you a place in his court. You will become his heir."

A glowing dark maroon shaft emerged in Carman's hand. Frosty energy sparked around its point. "If you wish to live another day, shut your sister up and show her who's in control."

"Our father is weak. His blood is dead in my veins."

Dain, with his stern, broad, prominent cheekbones, jutted out his chin. His face belied the cruelty in his eyes, the coldness of hatred seeping through his pores.

"You will lose to me. I promise you, a day will come when you three will bow at my feet." I added a slight smile of defiance.

His eyes were hard and filled with dislike.

"Diablo of the celestial realm will rule, and the dark overlords will take control of the realms. Stand with us, my sister. I will grant power beyond your belief once we destroy the kundalini." Dain leaned in so close his lips almost touched me.

Had Uriel survived? My heart felt Uriel's love within, and I took pleasure in the feeling of connection. "Never will I live on the dark side."

"Enough of this squabble. Walk over the bridge and bring me the book."

Carman's tone scratched with irritation. I felt the surrounding bonds disappear. I stretched my hands in front of me, hoping to buy myself some time. Cocked my head, I huffed a sneering laugh. Then, I removed the pack from my back. "Come and get it." I intended to goad Carman into making a mistake or unblocking my powers.

"Dain, bring her to me."

His hand grabbed my arm.

With my slave ring, I grasped his magic source. I pulled his magic and conjured a removal spell.

The energy poured into my body, and I absorbed his magic and broke the hindrance spell.

"Stealing another's power. Smart. But Dain is no novice. He'll recover from your theft, and you'll lose a piece of your soul as payment." Carman shuffled toward me, her brow raised.

I cringed, knowing that using his magic blackened my heart.

The dead finally rose from their kneeling and moved closer.

I glanced around. If any of them came after me, I'd be toast. Instead, I reached for Uriel's bond to find the courage I needed to prove my power over Carman's.

I tapped into Carman's body but couldn't locate the ribbons of her magic. My instincts stirred, my senses lifting to the next level of acuity, and I imagined her special gifts. The slave ring vibrated in the pure darkness. Fear stabbed into me, and I broke away, seeing the corruption and desire in her eyes. She wanted me to touch and taste her strength.

"You can't cross into this level." Leaving the metal container on the bridge, I backed away, watching to see what she would do next.

"Sluguro Pestendo."

A teal complex weave enveloped the box. It moved from the bridge and settled right in front of Carman.

She drew her sword from the sheath hanging over her back. "Secure her." Carman shouted to the masses of ghostly people.

Hundreds of men and women stormed the bridge.

I ran. I could never defeat them all. A wink of metal flashed, and my slave ring became a scimitar. I huffed and beheaded two of them before jabbing another in the stomach. Four more came toward me like a mindless mob. At least they didn't have knives. But soon, they'd exhaust me. I changed my scimitar into a whip and called to Uriel, hoping he'd feel the anxiety scouring through me. I lassoed the nearest zombie. As soon as I disposed of one group, another came.

I heard the roar of the crowd, and men on horseback charged through the portal. The dark elves and dwarves battled in a bloodbath. I dodged more attacks, swirling the living dead into a massive pile of sliced-up halves as their torsos flopped.

Dub, the darkest, used the zombies as a shield and moved in to grasp my wrist and drag me to the bridge. Pushing me to my knees, he yanked my hair. "Open the case."

"No." I spat right into his face.

His fist punched my jaw, and blood spurted from my mouth.

I fought the pain and pushed away the lightheadedness.

Carman pointed to one of her groveling dead men to open the case.

The lock didn't budge as the man ran his hands over the surface looking for a hidden latch.

"Those who created the original spell must release the protective shield."

"Dother, open that damn box." Carman's golden eyes blazed with anger.

I held my breath, and my whole body vibrated with energy.

Dother picked up the chest and pried at the seal with his blade. A vapor of green haze swirled around him. In seconds, he collapsed to the ground.

When she kneeled next to Dother, Carman's mental shields disappeared. The venom wove itself around him like a cocoon.

"Send the book," I demanded.

Dub, in the shadows of darkness, moved behind Carman and whispered in her ear.

"Give me the elixir." Carman's stony gaze penetrated like hot pokers of steel.

I laughed in disbelief at the despair on my mother's face. I honestly couldn't believe she really loved her sons. Weakness. I hardened and couldn't allow myself to feel empathy toward any of them.

"Give me the book." Fury fueled my voice and marked my every word.

"Let him suffer. It makes no difference. Look around, Mother. Dead people grovel at your feet. Now I'll take the only thing you love—your sons."

"Do whatever you want. Their lives mean little to me." Carman gave away nothing in her tone.

"You've already revealed your love, so don't play like his life doesn't matter."

She stood, turned her back to me, and faced the living dead. They all bowed in reverence before she turned back and narrowed her eyes. "If you value Brigit and Katrina's lives, give me the remedy."

"All I want is the jewel. Keep the book." I stood confidently and refused to allow her threats to intimidate me.

"The jewel for Dother's life. He might have five more minutes before the venom steals his last breath." I crept my arm around in taunting movements. "Since he's already here in Niflheim, he'll be right at home."

"The jewel is yours. Step over the bridge into regret."

I wavered, staring into the prison where she'd held my father captive. With one foot in, I risked never escaping the bonds. If Carman had changed places with me, everyone would have lost. I had to stop her. The red jasper meant people's lives. I crossed the bridge, and the sounds of the fighting ceased.

"Give me the antidote."

"No."

I removed the antique box from the metal container and took out the grimoire of maps. I handed Carman the book. "Remove the spell and give me the gem."

"Soforus, adrarus, I am the spell-caster, release the red jasper and return to the child of fate," Carman hissed. "Now, save Dother."

The red jasper materialized in my hand. I reached into my boot and removed the antidote.

Carman snatched the bottle.

Dub aimed his sword, ready to strike me dead.

Time collided with itself. I saw Uriel charge into Niflheim. His fury raged through him, and I felt his angst.

Using the power within my soul, I poured my heart into him. "I love you."

Behind my back, I reached for Odin's spear and hurled it at Dub. The man's eyes widened, and his hands grasped the spear sticking out of his shoulder.

The wall vanished.

Uriel lifted me into his arms and dashed for the bridge.

"The book. Get the book." Uriel released me and took the grimoire from where Carman had dropped it.

Whirlwinds of spells swirled, creating a magical storm. The dead who idolized her ran in fear, their homes collapsing into dust. Earthquakes erupted. I followed Uriel to the bridge, but the veil closed behind him. I pounded my hands in despair, realizing my mother had trapped me here in regret.

Feeling rooted to the spot, I had to risk the dark magic and face her, or she'd always control my actions. I raised my hand, and sang the necromancer song of the dead, and pulled her power from her.

Skuld's voice sang into my thoughts. "Just like you build a cake one layer at a time, you win some battles through small, incremental victories."

Leave it to the Norn goddess to use my own metaphors to prove a point.

Carman frantically used spells to ease Odin's spear from Dub's body.

If I attacked and stole her magic, I would become her. I was better than the darkness that lived in her heart.

Compassion.

If I lost what made me who I was—then she won. My ability to soothe pain and share beautiful emotions lived in my soul. I dropped the Death Song.

I reached into my pouch and closed my fingers around the pebble Hel gave me to call on her.

Hel appeared at the realm's portal, and Odin's spear vanished.

The doorway opened onto Alfheim. My father stepped into Niflheim and took my hand.

"Freyr, I fight on the side of light. My debt is now paid to you for the suffering you endured." Hel disappeared, and Niflheim faded from view.

My father jerked me into his embrace as the portal closed.

I flung my arms around him and wept. Uriel and I had accomplished our task. We'd raised the kundalini, and I had the gem.

Chapter Twenty-Three

URIEL

Uriel

I entered Kumuria and headed to the archangel crystal towers with my hands in my pockets. I scanned the room, feeling the intense responsibility of helping each of my brothers succeed. The scar beneath my breastbone faded, replaced with the mark of the dragon. Since my mate and I placed the red jasper with citrine into the Muladhara of the Kundalini Shakti, we'd survived the first challenge. With the root established, this created a foundation for the ruling princes to combat the darkness threatening the pantheons.

"The supernatural wars have started." Archangel Mikael leaned against one of the majestic columns in the tower's community room.

"In my visit with Valefor, he mentioned legions of demons are choosing sides." Luc tapped his own breastplate. "Small scrimmages have broken out. Ananiel says that half of the fallen angels have sided with Diablo, hoping to regain power. They have a taste for revenge against Yahweh for their banishment."

I turned to Mikael and clenched a fist. "We're repeating the first angelic wars with bigger consequences."

"What about Ananiel? Whose side will he fight for?" Zadkiel asked.

He and Lucifer both had justifiable reasons to want our father to suffer, but if we lost, the twelve princes faced the true death, always doomed to live in purgatory without the completion of our souls.

"Ananiel and I will align ourselves with Yahweh. Our father's agreed that the watchers will receive their rightful positions in Kumuria." Luc smiled at me.

Lucifer was the light of a new day and would be the last of the princes. Confidence filled me that Brigit was his mate. The future years held a challenge that invigorated the warrior in us all.

"Ananiel's been a fair ruler of the watchers. What of the Nephilim children?" Rafael sat with his arms across the back of the chair.

He watched me, since I was one of the Throne angels of the courts who had voted to alienate the Nephilim to Oceania.

"That's still a problem." Mikael went to the table and picked up one of Moira's cherry tarts.

"How will Ananiel handle the issue that the rulers still refuse to treat our angelic children as anything but human guardians? They want acknowledgement as deities." Gabriel turned to Metatron, the one of us in daily communication with Ananiel.

Dressed casually in blue jeans and a dark emerald polo shirt, Metatron placed an arm on the back of the sectional. Born of human parents, he understood the Nephilim dilemma.

"Yesterday, word came through the telecom leading into Oceania that Poseidon has agreed to join forces with Ananiel. I'm waiting to hear from Hades. A chance of a split in their ranks." Zadkiel walked over to the telescreen and turned on the monitor displaying the ocean. "I believe the next prince will be Ananiel. He's always been the most wounded of us."

"The withholding of our mates for so many centuries has created an emotional isolation, leaving each of us vulnerable." Gabriel, the heart of the angel realm, pulled back his arrow and let it fly into the holographic images. "Ananiel needs a chance to heal his wounded soul."

I understood their distress and desire. Now that I'd found Moira, I couldn't imagine living one more day without her. Carman's setback wouldn't last before she caused more problems.

"Ananiel's strength lives within the sacral chakra of water. Oceania will rise and take its place in society. "The gods' offspring will serve as guardians of the land." Zadkiel turned off the telecom.

Luc put his arm over my shoulder. "Let's head home. A very feisty redhead has some explaining to do."

"Brigit's a hellcat. Have fun."

"Oh, I plan on it."

I understood that never again did I want Moira separated from me. And based on the way Luc watched Brigit, it was only a matter of time before he realized she was his archeia.

Chapter Twenty-Four
EPILOGUE:MOIRA

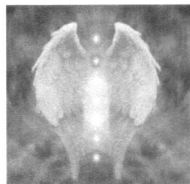

A week passed since Uriel and I consummated our love. Tonight I would join the Seidr priestesses. I scanned the audience, looking for Uriel, and our gazes locked. A sizzling awareness of raw sexual heat thrummed through me. I couldn't wait until the ceremony was over and I was back in his arms. Standing with two other women under the energy of the full moon.

Freya took each of my hands. "Moira, daughter of Freyr, Seidr leader of the priestess witches, you have earned your magical stave. I proclaim you the sentinel leader in my court." A feeling that I could conquer the world filled me. My father's dream was for me to be one of Alfheim's priestesses.

To honor my family and community, I shared my epic Kalevala poem: Long, long ago, when the world was new, the species all got along. Then, the greed for dominance arose, dividing the clans into individual pantheons ruled with their separate gods.

Uriel joined me, taking my trembling hand in his. Our story was the beginning, and twelve others would continue the epic. Silence prevailed, with not a dry eye in the room. Uriel kissed me and left the platform.

The clouds opened to reveal Yahweh, Odin, Zeus, and many gods of the other dimensions.

"Bringer of light and fire, your magic honors Kumuria." His voice slipped over my mind like crushed velvet, giving me the confidence I'd need to lead the Seidr priestesses in this challenging time.

In the clouds, a ribbon of gold spiraled into various mystical creatures representing one and all the pantheons of people. The dragon hovered behind the gods.

My father stepped onto the stage and handed me my stave. My eyes widened at the intricate runic symbols along the willow wood shaft. Each rune told the story of my life and courtship with Uriel. Amber jewels, herbs of magic, and a scent of honeycomb for my baking filled the three core centers of the runic symbols. I gasped.

My father continued, "Daughter of my blood, the Norns have blessed us with the gift of your life. Honor it well and lead our people in the battle against the darkness. Your light will be a beacon for others to follow. The Norns of fate have chosen you to be the mistress and foundation of all the pantheons."

My father's words seeped deep into my soul. Looking over the academy gardens, I gazed at friends, acquaintances, and fellow conspirators. Part of me wanted to teleport back to Sierra Madre, where everyone just stopped by for my special crumb cakes or a cup of coffee. Taking a deep breath, I pushed all else from my mind. "Elfin clan of Alfheim, I stand here at the podium of Mythos Academy of the Supernatural on this day of the blue moon with so much pride in my heart. I have pride in the elfin people who supported and honored me with the highest of esteem."

"You're the best." Valefor and his legion of demons all cheered.

Silvercrest and Dhubagret wore the sunniest smiles, and I knew those two had engraved the runes into the willow wood.

"Your stave has chosen you, a woman of integrity." My father took me in his arms. The roaring crowd sang my praises. Feeling overwhelmed, I chewed my lower lip, hoping I'd live up to their expectations.

I went to my table and took a seat next to my father. I gazed around the room. My two best friends sat among the ruling Sarim princes of Kumuria. Luc and Brigit were in a furious debate.

I smiled, listening to the jovial conversations as bits of gossip made their way to the priestess' table. Adoration lived in their voices and hearts that I was the mother of the kundalini. I would help each of Uriel's brothers fulfill their obligations until the twelve gemstones of the kundalini shone above the cosmos, securing the light for generations to come.

My mate sent silent messages. "For dessert, I require your sweet buttercream mounds."

"Stop, I'm focusing on Freya's speech."

"Mmn, I can't wait to lick at the icing first, then take tiny nibbles until the cake disappears in sweet satisfaction."

"You're awful." This man seared every live wire in my body. I'd never stay away from him for long. "I love you."

"My wild, courageous baker, the woman who healed my soul, I love you too!"

I twirled the citrine quartz on my left finger. The ring symbolized the connection of kindred mates. I lifted my glass of champagne the waiter poured for the toast and gazed into the flame of Uriel's eyes. "To us."

Storm Warrior Book Two

As an archangel and the head of the Grigori watchers, a clan tasked with protecting humanity from its own worst impulses, I don't have time to indulge in relationships, much less with mortals. I am well aware of the irony of saving a woman's life by binding my soul to her. But little did I realize she was my archeia.

Also by Jaylee Austin

Good day peeps,

If you'd like to be part of my review or beta team, email me at https://jayleeauthor@jayleeaustin.com

Visit my website to receive insightful information about Jaylee's world. To enjoy a free book, join my mailing list visit https://linktr.ee/JayleesWorld

To help support me on my journey, join my exclusive Substack.

https://biancareeves.substack.com

Reviews are the lifeblood of an author. If you've enjoyed your reading experience, please leave a review.

I always enjoy hearing from you.

To all those readers who believe in the happily ever after, I write for you. A writer is powerful. We create people who are so real they break your heart. The world created by a writer becomes the dreams of other people. By the power of writing, monsters can transform into heroes and princesses into assassins.

Marvelous stories provoke emotions with their words, but it's the reader who falls in love with our world and shares a moment within our hearts.

Thank you for your support, your insight, and your commitment to reading a good story.

Monster in Moonlight Series

Labyrinth's Heart 2025

Coming Soon Book Two: Rex's Story

Cursed Connections: Coming out April 2026

New Monster Series

Satyr romances coming soon

The Return of the Draugr Series: Monster gothic romance

Shadows of the Harvest Moon

Shadows of the Yuletide 2026

Light of the Beltane Fires 2027

Light of Midsummer's Eve 2027

Christmas Magic Series

Heart Stone Magic Coming October 2026

Contemporary Stand Alone

Dragonfly Heart

Valentine Angel-Novella

Sedona Series

Fairy Rose

Emerald's Cove

Agartha

Omnibus Set

Travel Through Time: All three books of the Sedona saga

Sarim Prince Series of the Archangel Universe

Magically Delicious

Storm Warrior

The Watcher's Guild

Bound by Destiny

Coming Soon Tattooed Justice in 2026

Omnibus Set

The Power of Love: The first three books

Spin-off series (Supernatural archangel Universe)

Yellowstone Wolf

Yellowstone Cougar

Coming soon Yellowstone Bear in 2026

Each of the books in The Sarim Prince and the spin-off series are books with their own romantic love story. But to have a perfect reader experience, I suggest reading the books in order to gain understanding of the universe in which the characters live. But it isn't necessary if reading for just the romance or adventure.

Book 1 Magically Delicious: Sarim prince series

Book 2 Storm Warrior: Sarim prince series

Book 2.5 Yellowstone Wolf: Archangel universe

Book 3 The Watcher's Guild: Sarim prince series

Book 3.5 Yellowstone Cougar: Archangel universe

Book 4 Bound By Destiny: Sarim prince series

Book 5 Tattooed Justice: Sarim prince series

Book 5.5 Yellowstone Bear: Archangel universe coming in 2027

Anthology and now released as a short story

The Spirit of Love: **A Timeless Curse** (Historical Time Travel)

The Light of Love: **The Snow Stag** (Historical Time Travel)

The Lure of Hunt: **Chasing Destiny** (A Sci-Fi Cyborg Romance)

Love Me in Vegas: Kickstarter/Author Nation: All or Nothing

About the Author

In a whimsical corner of the universe that echoes the enchanting realms of Wonderland, Jaylee Austin weaves tales that dance between the ethereal and the imaginative. Enthralled by mythology from every dimension—be it the enchanting Celtic goddesses, the vast treks through the nine worlds of the Nordic realms, or the ancient whispers of the Sumerian gods—she crafts modern romantic worlds that shimmer with magical realism.

Her desk, a canvas of creativity, is often interrupted by the playful pounces of her two adorable companions, but none more so than Tilly, her clever black pug. A true companion on her literary adventures, Tilly offers sage wisdom as they both ponder the mysterious questions that tug at the hearts of readers.

With a spirited background as a retired high school English and Theater teacher, Jaylee brought wit and warmth to the classroom, inspiring countless students to embrace their own creativity during National Writing Month. Through her enchanting stories, Jaylee invites readers to leap into alternate realities where the ordinary becomes extraordinary, and every page is a step further down the rabbit hole.

https://linktr.ee/JayleesWorld